SPIKED!

SPIKED!

Bob Madison

PRESS

Published by Vulpine Press in the United Kingdom in 2022

ISBN: 978-1-83919-480-1

www.vulpine-press.com

For Charles and Mirella
Who laugh at my jokes. Sometimes.

Chapter One

So this is the story of me and A.J. Lopez.

We are now just about to start college, and I wanted to get everything down that came before, in case I forget it.

As if I could.

It all began when we were born. I'm two weeks older than A.J., and he's been trying to catch up ever since. Our parents lived next door to each other, and when we were infants, we were placed in the same playpen.

So I've known A.J. my whole life. Minus those two weeks, of course.

We grew up in Stony Brook, which is a town on Long Island. It was a great place to grow up. It felt like a small town, but we were just about two hours away from New York City by train. Not that we got to New York all that much until we were teenagers. But still.

Stony Brook is one of those places filled with trees and those houses that adults call "charming". My charming house was next to A.J.'s charming house (as I've said), and there was a huge elm tree between the two of them. When we got older, we were able to climb out of our bedroom windows and sneak into each other's bedrooms. When my father found out about it, I thought he would kill me. He didn't.

Actually, I didn't think my father would kill me. He's not that type of guy. But more on that later.

So there we were, in the playpen together. Legend has it that the first fight we ever had was when we were around one year old. We were both in the playpen, and A.J. was playing with a plastic toy hammer. He decided to hit me with it, so I decided to bite him.

Now, both of us were too young to remember this, but it's a story that our mothers love to pull out for reasons that have never been clear to me. As for whether it is true or not, all I can say is that the biting part sounds like me. Come to think of it, the hammer part sounds like A.J. Let's just say it's true and call it a day.

Talking of mothers brings me back to fathers (funny how that works), and parents in general…

A.J.'s mother is wonderful. She was born in Honduras, on a farm, believe it or not. She knows all kinds of things that no one else ever seems to know, like when the birds are coming back in the spring or where to find the fish back when A.J. and I liked fishing. Her name is Lourdes, but I've always called her mom.

She is one of those small four-by-four moms, nearly as wide as she is short, and with a big beaming face. I think she's terrific, but sometimes A.J. disagrees. You know how kids are.

A.J.'s father is a real piece of work. He is tall and stands like his spine is one single unbending piece of metal. He has thick brows and a heavy mustache that nearly blots out his disapproving mouth. I've been telling him jokes all my life and he's never laughed once. Not that this makes him all that different from anyone else…

He is from Ecuador and is the manager of a chain of retail stores found all over Long Island. I have always resisted his offers for a summer job in one of them. His name is Fernando and I call him Mr. Lopez.

I love my own mother just as much as I love A.J.'s, except, of course, A.J.'s mother never grounded me or took away my PlayStation when I "had too much". But even with those significant faults, my mother has been a good one all around.

She is around the same age as A.J.'s mother (I guess) and where Lourdes is small, my mom is tall. Her name is Marion and she has very pale skin that highlights her vibrant red hair. She has two watery and very blue eyes that seem to hover over you like a benevolent cloud. She is a great cook, if heavy on the meat and potatoes, and once had hopes that I would someday become a priest. I don't think that's in the cards, as you will see, but all of us are entitled to our dreams, even if it's to control other people's lives. Our mothers would often go to church together, but I don't think A.J.'s mother ever wanted him to become a priest. Make of that what you will.

My dad is a real character, and he plays a big part in the story I'm going to tell. His name is Edward, but I have never heard anyone call him anything other than Eddie. He is a cartoonist working for various newspapers and even sometimes advertising agencies. He works from home, drawing a political cartoon for the local rag every day, even though I have never heard him discuss politics once.

He is a smallish guy—when I was fourteen I already had a couple of inches on him—and is the type you see smiling benignly from behind a cardigan sweater. He makes Mr. Rogers look like the Incredible Hulk, and I have no idea what A.J.'s dad thinks of him. (Actually, I have an idea, but, frankly, to hell with A.J.'s dad.) I'll tell you this, though, when it comes to Old Mans, I got A.J. beat easy.

Oh. And he laughs at my jokes. Mostly. He scores big points there.

Sadly, neither A.J. nor I are only children. Funny how that works. Only children always go around saying they wish they had brothers and sisters. People with brothers and sisters always go around wishing they were only children. Ever wonder why that is?

Both of us have sisters, though they couldn't be more different.

A.J.'s sister, Lupe, is a good ten years older than both of us. The great thing about her is that she has only been moderately annoying and interfering. When A.J. and I were both little, Lupe would often make a big fuss about having to babysit for us, but we never understood what all the drama was about. We'd sit on the couch and watch television while she was on the phone with her friends. But the way she told it, you would think the world was coming to an end.

The best part of the situation, though, was that I was able to do a great imitation of her talking on the phone. I would do this for A.J. and he would laugh until his eyes grew wet. Of course, one day Lupe caught me and she smacked me until my eyes grew wet. I guess that's fair.

My sister, Nancy, is only two years younger than me and A.J., and has been the bane of our existence. We would want to go out and play around, ride our bikes or do PlayStation, and Mom would always ask, "Why don't you boys include Nancy?"

Because who wants to include their kid sister? I would think, but never say out loud.

Our houses are pretty much what you would expect. We both have three-bedroom homes, which makes two-kids per family very workable. (We have a friend, Preston, who is one of five kids, and his house is huge. A.J. and I first made friends with him so we could play around his massive house.

Turns out he was a pretty great guy and Preston is a big part of this story too.) When we got older, both A.J. and I wanted to convert our basements into our respective bedrooms, but that never seemed to happen. There was a period when we wanted to build a treehouse, too, and my dad bought the lumber and even drew plans for it. At the rate we are going, though, A.J. and I will collect Social Security before we ever build it.

That's a shame. My dad really wanted a treehouse. I'll never be a priest and I'll never build the tree house. Not even in college, and already weighted with failure.

I guess this is the time to tell you a little bit about myself. And A.J., aside from the stuff I've already told you, I mean.

A.J. has always been taller, and now stands a good four inches higher than me. And I've been trying to catch up ever since (Have I used that joke already?). He has very thick dark hair that he combs back and large, liquid brown eyes. He's got one of those square jaws that you could use for an anvil (if you turned his head upside down) and tiny ears that look like mushrooms popping out of the side of his head.

He was always in great shape, even when we were little kids. He had to start shaving when we were in middle school. He's got those strong forearms that seem to have muscular veins running through them (Who has muscular veins?). His hands are big and powerful and his feet often smell.

The best things about him are that he looked out for me when we were growing up and always laughed at my jokes. In school, he was something of a doofus compared to me, but he was the better man in every way. He was unfailingly kind, always generous, and the type of guy who makes friends and never seems to have enemies. If he was more dishonest, he'd make a great politician. If he had a nasty streak, he'd made a great bully. Fortunately, he was none of those things, and just ended up making a great A.J.

By the way, the A.J. stands for Alberto Javier. No one calls him Alberto Javier. His teachers, his parents, his friends, his sister, me, everyone calls him A.J. If Curley— that's his dog—could talk, he'd call him A.J., too.

One last thing about A.J.: he's got one of those smiles like the floodlights you see at Hollywood premieres. I used to joke that I had to put on sunglasses when he smiled at me.

And then there's me. You're stuck with me for the duration of this story, so you should know a little more about me.

My name is Thom Wilcox, and yes, that first name is spelled correctly. It's like Thomas, but without the AS, and is pronounced Tom and not Thumb. And why my parents did this to me is another one of life's mysteries that I'll never understand.

I got my mother's red hair and blue eyes and pale skin. That means summers running around with A.J. have left me deeply freckled (Thanks, Mom). Like my mom, I'm also big, not tall, but powerfully built for someone who is average size. Where most redheads have lanky hair, mine tends towards the thick and bushy. Nancy once said that she read somewhere that guys with bushy red hair as kids would one day go bald. I saw this as another good reason to push her out of my room. I only shave about twice a week and, let me tell you, that kills me.

I do pretty well in school and have always been really good at English. As you can tell from that Lord of the Rings episode with my mom, I like to read. I'm the only kid who would put down the PlayStation if I thought there was a really good book to be read. Go figure.

Even though I looked strong, I seemed to attract a lot of bullies growing up. A.J. always managed to swat most of them away, but every now and then they would get to me. I was also one of those kids who spent a lot of time with grown-ups, and when grown-ups get talking, you get to hear a lot of strange stuff if you only keep listening.

So now you have everything you need to know to read this story. It's about me and A.J.: how we grew up, how we changed, and—well, I might as well get this out of the way now—how we came to love one another. It's not a "gay story", at least, not in the way you're expecting. Read it and see.

When I'm done with it all, I'll tell you what I think is going to happen next. Of course, you can turn to the end of the book and read that part now, but I'll save you the trouble. We're about to start college and this is all that came before that. We all live happily ever after (mostly) and we're going to have to grow older before we figure out what happens next. There. Spoiled it for you.

And now, to tell this properly, I have to go back to when we were really little kids.

Chapter Two

So, we go to school.

I think most stories begin when you're in school (Okay, I guess they start when you're born, but if I can't remember biting A.J. in the playpen, then I'm not going to remember that. Right?).

School is supposed to be where you learn about the world and discover what kind of person you are. And, if you're lucky, what kind of people your friends are. It doesn't always work out like that, but, all-in-all, I was pretty lucky.

Both of our moms decided that it was best for us (and, it turned out, our sisters) to go to Catholic school. There was only one Catholic grade school in Stony Brook, and that was St. Benedict.

Now, neither A.J. nor I went to preschool. I know, I know. Almost everybody goes to preschool. But A.J.'s mom did translation work for the local college (Spanish-to-English), and my mom didn't work at all, so they just decided to keep us home until kindergarten. Also, my mother would say that we boys would be socialized because we had each other to play with. That's the kind of thing my mother always says. Reality does have a way of catching up with her.

So, like I said, I was pretty lucky, though the very first day of school I stood there and cried before our mothers left. Fortunately A.J. took my hand and we walked in together. For that first year or so, everyone thought we were brothers, despite the fact that we looked nothing alike and A.J. was the only kid in kindergarten with a five o'clock shadow.

You had to wear a uniform at St. Benedict. A white shirt and school tie with gray pants and black shoes for boys, and this green-and-white plaid skirt for girls. A.J. would grow out of his uniform like a weed in rainy season, and I would get his hand-me-downs.

One of the earliest memories I have of school was Valentine's Day in the first grade. We were taught by a nun, Sister Thereselle (we called her Sister Terrible Smell), and she suggested that we pass out Valentine's Day cards to our classmates. I hadn't really made a lot of friends by first grade, so the only one I passed out was to A.J. I signed it "Love, Thom" and called it a day.

Well, A.J. got tons of them (of course). When he opened mine, some of the other kids told him that boys didn't send Valentines to other boys, and if they did send Valentines to other boys, they didn't sign them "love".

Now, I was just a dope in this case. I figured everyone sent Valentines to people they knew and signed everything "love" (except, maybe report cards). One of A.J.'s friends told him to give it back to me and have me cross out "love", which he did and I did. I crossed out "love" and put "See you." Whether this was an improvement of any sort is an open question.

I wasn't angry or embarrassed by this. I just shrugged.

One of the kids who made A.J. bring the card back was Robert Dillworth. He was pretty much a jerk in first grade, and now that we've been through grade school and high school together, I could tell you that he is still pretty much a jerk now. He was short, strong and nasty, with broad shoulders even in first grade and blond hair tousled over an angry face. Fortunately, with a name like Dillworth, I was able to make him suffer almost as much as he made me.

For instance, it was the practice of Sister Terrible Smell to have us pass our homework down the row we were sitting in, and she would pick them up at the first desk of each row. When Dillworth got my homework to pass down, he always crumpled it up.

This went on for weeks until Sister Terrible Smell asked, in front of the whole class, "Thom, why is your homework always such a mess?"

"Sister," I said, always ready to let my mouth get me in trouble, "that's because Robert Dill*weed* always crumples it up when I pass it down."

She tilted her head to one side (she always did. I think the rocks in her head were all piled to the right), "Who?"

"Robert Dill*wanker*. You know," I pointed down the aisle, "the one who always has snot coming out of his nose."

Needless to say, that did not go over well with Sister Terrible Smell or Dillworth. She yelled at him for crumpling my homework, and then yelled at me for being rude. Go figure.

Dillworth will show up in this story now and then, but he's more of a background annoyance than anything else (like farting). But the real piece of luck to come out of the St. Valentine's Day massacre was that I made a new friend, Matthew Preston.

Preston (everyone called him Preston, I'll bet his mother called him Preston) was one of those quiet guys who saw everything. He didn't miss a thing. Growing up he was usually about my height and medium weight, with dark hair and those dark rimmed glasses that were popular ever since Harry Potter. He had a roundish and serious face, and his mouth relaxed into a natural frown.

But he wasn't really frowning on the inside. That was just how he looked. And, like I said, he saw *everything*.

Once Dillworth went back to his seat with the other guys, Preston, who was sitting next to me and had never said a word to me before, turned to me and said, "They're just kids."

They're just kids? This was only first grade and Preston had already distanced himself above the fray. Preston was in many ways the most important person at school to both me and A.J. We would each have friends—friends we shared and friends we had separately—but Preston was the guy who somehow put everything into context for us.

Well, we made our way through the early grades without too much drama. A.J. was better at science and math than I was (a monkey is better at math than I was), while I did really, really well in English, history and religion. Preston did well in *everything*.

***

I learned several things during eighth grade, our last year at St. Benedict, and one of them was that I don't like to be pushed around, no matter who does it.

It was Sr. Terrible Smell who managed to teach me that one. I was standing in the school hallway, talking to my science and math teacher about a school-wide event I was organizing. Something grabbed me from behind, pulled me away and spun me around.

It was Sr. Terrible Smell, furious bits of spittle at the corners of her mouth.

"How dare you eavesdrop when adults are talking?!"

Oozing all the icy disdain I could muster at twelve, I raised an eyebrow (something that took me weeks to master at the bathroom mirror), and sneered, "We were having a conversation and they wanted my opinion."

Terrible Smell turned to the math and science teachers, who were standing there, opened mouthed. Terrible Smell turned without a word and vanished.

I could never tell if the two teachers thought I should have stood up for myself or not, they never mentioned it. But I made note of it to myself, and stood a little taller after that.

It was Preston who identified what A.J. and I were at heart: nerds.

Our nerdishness flowered thanks again to my dad. During the September that eighth grade started, Dad told me he would need me one Saturday afternoon and that I should have A.J. with me.

We had no idea what he wanted until he ushered us down into the basement (my dad could make a mystery out of buying an ice cream cone). He had set up a home theater down there, complete with tiered seating. He pointed us to seats and told us to "shut up and be happy".

A.J. turned to me and shrugged as the basement theater lights dimmed.

Next thing we knew, there was a blare of trumpets and *Star Wars* started.

A.J. sighed and I groaned. Loudly. Then I tried the raised eyebrow, but I think it was now too dark in there to work.

It's not that we never heard of *Star Wars*—how could you escape it? —it's just that we were never into it. I mean, it's just an old movie and who cares?

"Just watch," my dad said. And we did.

Star Wars was like a nuclear explosion in our brains. We had both seen lots of superhero movies and tons of action flicks, but *this* was something else. We sat quiet, amazed. At one point, Nancy came in, took a look at the screen and left with a snort. We paid no attention.

When it was all over, dad told me about how it really was a call back to science fiction movies from the thirties, and also World War II movies and even Westerns (he says things like that). But we didn't care. We cared about that place a long time ago in a galaxy far, far away.

A.J. and I talked about it all weekend. A rebellion of farm boys and scoundrels and princesses against an evil galactic empire. What's not to love? We kept wondering how big the Empire was, and how they would recover from the loss of the Death Star and if Han Solo was going to stick around long enough to make a difference.

The whole thing especially lit up A.J.'s imagination. I had the feeling that *Star Wars* showed him that there was more to the world he knew and life as he lived it. At least, I *think*.

It was Preston, of course, who made it even more real. We were talking to him about the movie at lunch that Monday, and he had seen all of them and could quote chapter and verse. ("It gets verse?" I asked. No one laughed.) He told us that we would have to watch the rest of the movies before we "were even equipped to have an intelligent conversation", but he dropped tantalizing hints about what would happen next.

Of course, we got dad to show us the second one, *The Empire Strikes Back*, the next Saturday. If anything, that left us more excited. Ending with Han Solo frozen and taken away by pirates, and Luke Skywalker finding out that the evil Darth Vader was really his father, this was a movie that had a sense of urgency that we had not shared before.

At that point, we abandoned Dad and started looking for the rest of the series on our own. Preston told us that the third movie, *The Return of the Jedi*, would clean up the loose ends for us, and that we had to see that before we moved onto the next trilogy. (He also told us the next trilogy took place *before* the one we saw. It made no sense to me—and still doesn't—but who am I to argue with a galactic empire?)

Dad grudgingly gave me his Blu-ray of that for A.J. and I to catch when we had a chance. We just could not wait for next Saturday. That Tuesday, Preston was over at my place, going over algebra of all things, when A.J. called and said he was free, and we should come on over with the movie.

Preston and I went to his place and we started to watch the movie in A.J.'s basement.

He did not have a home theater, like we did, but A.J.'s basement had a heavy carpet, the old living room furniture that was upstairs until A.J.'s mom got new stuff, and the old television (ditto). A.J. and I sprawled on the floor while Preston sat up straight beside us, his back resting on the bottom of the couch.

Neither A.J. nor I liked it as much as the first two, and Preston did not help by saying, "watch, this is important" every few moments, as if this was another piece of algebra we had to piece together. But we were delighted to see the Empire crumble, and, best of all, to see Luke come up against the Emperor.

As the credits were rolling, A.J. yelled, "Ewok!" and jumped me. We were wrestling, rolling all over the carpet with Preston sitting by, probably patiently thinking to himself *they're just kids*, when Mr. Lopez came down the stairs.

The wrestling stopped instantly, and the fun was sucked out of the room in a heartbeat. Preston, never at a loss, said, "Good afternoon, Mr. Lopez".

Mr. Lopez paid no attention to him.

"Alberto Javier," he said, looking at A.J. "What are you doing?"

"We were just watching *Return of the Jedi*," I started.

"I asked my son."

"We were just watching *Return of the Jedi*," A.J. said. I wondered if it sounded any better coming from him.

"What did I ask you to do today?"

A.J. looked at me and then at Preston, as if he expected us to know. Finally he looked at his dad and shrugged, not knowing.

"You were supposed to clean out the garage. It is not cleaned." He gestured around the room with his hand. "Instead, I come home to find *this*."

He made *this* sound as if we were burning down orphanages and using the flames to light cigars. I thought about raising an eyebrow and giving Mr. Lopez a taste of sneering condescension (I had gotten very good at it), but decided against it. Instead, I looked at Preston and then at Mr. Lopez. "I'm sorry. Didn't know. We just came to watch television."

Mr. Lopez pointed at Preston and then at me. "You two. Out."

You didn't have to tell Preston twice. He rose, said, "See you later, A.J" and went up the stairs. I got on my hind legs and asked, "Can I help clean out the garage?"

"You are not my son," Mr. Lopez said.

Thank God for small favors, I thought. I shrugged. "Just trying to help."

"See you at school, Thom," A.J. said. I went up the stairs thinking *I* hadn't done anything wrong—*we* hadn't done anything wrong—and that parents could sure be jerks.

Home, I went to my room and pulled out my PlayStation, but my heart wasn't in it. I was lying down in bed with my hands under my head when I heard the clanging. I went to the window for a look.

Outside, despite that it was already getting dark, A.J. was hauling bikes and junk out of the garage prior to giving it a good cleaning. I thought he would be at it for the next few hours, but didn't dare come out and offer to help.

That night at dinner, Dad asked if we had caught *Return of the Jedi*.

"Those movies are so stupid," Nancy said, ten at the time and picking at her food the way some people pick at their noses.

"Have you seen them?" Mom asked.

"No."

"Then you can't say anything about them, can you?"

Score one for Mom. I raised an eyebrow at Nancy in an effortless show of superiority.

Dad and I talked about the three movies. Because he's my dad, he spent a lot of time telling me about the Hero's Journey, and the mythic underpinnings of the story. He also said that it was all about how people find things bigger than themselves—a rebellion, The Force, the desire to right a wrong or a sense of quest—and how those big things help define them. Me, I just liked when things exploded.

Then I told them about A.J. getting in trouble. At first Mom and Dad didn't say anything, then Mom wiped her mouth and said, "Well, he should've cleaned the garage if he promised."

Somehow, I don't think that was the point of what I was trying to get at, but I left it alone. I know that through most of dinner I was thinking of poor A.J. having to clean out the garage alone, and how I wished I was there to help.

That's the thing about A.J. He's always kind and warm to others, but keeps himself to himself. There's a wall of privacy that even I hadn't penetrated at that time. It made him a great friend, but it also made him a challenge. We were best friends, but I was always looking for ways to make him like me even more. There was a lot of strength there, and I wanted some of it directed at me.

That night I heard A.J. pile everything neatly back into the garage while I was on my PlayStation and then go inside. I was up later than I should have been (tomorrow was a school day), and ended up in bed reading a book by Robert Heinlein that Preston pushed on me.

It was nearly midnight when I went to the window and looked across at A.J.'s house. All the lights were out except for his, and I could see his shadow moving around in his room.

And then, why I don't know, my eyes trailed along the branches of the elm tree that separated our houses.

This elm was enormous. I heard my dad say only a few weeks earlier that they would have to cut some of it back in case a hurricane came and blew it into the houses. I figured it would have to be a hell of a hurricane, because the tree was nearly as big and sturdy as a house itself. My eye ran along a branch that nearly brushed against my window and my eyes followed it to the trunk of the tree. Beyond that, another branch nearly tickled A.J.'s window.

Could I? I wondered.

I threw open the window and felt a blast of cold autumn night air grab me. I was just in a T-shirt and undershorts, so I went and grabbed a *Star Wars* hoodie that my dad gave me. I threw that on, put the hood over my head and poked a nervous foot outside of my window.

Now the branch under my window was more like a plank, and when I put my foot on it there was room to spare on either side of my toes. I reached out to some upper branches with both hands and planted my butt on the window sill.

My house is only two stories, but looking down at the grass below it felt like I was on top of the Empire State Building.

But, what can I say? I'm both cowardly and stupid. Holding both upper branches, I put my weight on the branch under my foot. It began to droop dangerously and I yelped in terror, but it only sagged an inch or two before getting stiff. I gulped and took another step.

And before I knew it, I had walked through the tree branches to the trunk of the tree. I was going to beat my chest like Tarzan and give a yell, but figured I was already pressing my luck.

Hugging the tree trunk, I scooted around the center and stepped onto the branch leading to A.J.'s room. I was relieved to find that the overhead branches I had to hold onto were even stronger on this side. I padded my way over the branch and made it to his window.

I could see A.J. sitting up in bed, reading. Holding onto a branch with my left hand to keep steady on my feet, I slowly lifted his window with my right.

I'll never forget the look on A.J.'s face. One minute, he's in bed looking down at his book. The next, he's looking up at his window, mouth open. I stepped into his room, pulled off the hood like a young Obi-Wan Kenobi and said, "I'm Luke Skywalker. I'm here to rescue you."

His face was blank for a moment and then he laughed like I never saw him laugh before.

And that was how we were able to see each other all the time. We now had a route to each other's rooms that we could use without our parents knowing, and we used it regularly.

First, we would sneak into each other's houses and do PlayStation when we were supposed to be asleep. But it got to be such a habit that we would even travel by tree when we had nothing special to do. There were weeks when we would sneak into each other's houses just to sit and read the *Star Wars* paperbacks that Preston had loaned us.

Of course, tree travel was not without setbacks. Nothing is. It would be a big part of the biggest hunk of trouble I bought in my last year at St. Benedict's.

This is what happened.

Right after the Christmas holidays, A.J. came down with a really bad cold. He was out of school for a few days, and I would bring him the homework every day. Then I'd do mine and do PlayStation or read until bedtime. I didn't have a lot of fun when A.J. wasn't around.

And school wasn't a lot of fun without him, either. I never realized until A.J. was gone how much we were a team, and how his popularity protected me from various jerks. Like Robert Dillworth.

While A.J. was gone, Dillworth would pass me every day in the lunchroom and rap on the back of my head hard with his knuckles. And he would laugh with his doofus friends, as if this was the funniest thing in the world.

Lots of the other guys noticed, but no one said anything. Even Preston just sat there, with that watchful face of his. I wonder if he was afraid that he would get some of the same if he said anything.

No matter. This went on for five days until that one Friday afternoon. I had already eaten and had my nose in Asimov's *Foundation* (which is pretty dull, actually), oblivious to everything around me. Next thing I know— *blam!*—a hard knuckle rap to the back of the head.

I turned and saw Robert Dillworth standing over me. His broad shoulders and mean ferret face were pretty intimidating, and I would've brushed it off, but some of the kids around me were snickering. The laughing hurt more than the knock on the head and I felt my face grow hot.

"Knock it off!" I said.

"Or what?" Dillworth took a chestful of air. "Faggot."

I know this sounds stupid, but the first thing I thought was, *a Jedi knight wouldn't put up with this crap.*

And the next thing I thought was, *and neither will I.*

Before I knew what I was doing, I stood up and faced him.

It was like that moment in *The Empire Strikes Back*: Luke Skywalker finally stands up to Darth Vader.

The table grew quiet. I could see Sister Terrible Smell at the far end of the cafeteria, doing something with the small kids. She didn't see anything. This was going to be interesting.

Before a word was said, Dillworth pushed me hard in the left shoulder with the palm of his hand. I don't know how I stayed on my feet, but I did.

I pushed him back. Hard.

He staggered back a step, his mouth tightening to a little slit.

I could feel the other kids watching us, like their eyes had weight.

Dillworth came back at me, pushing me even harder in the same spot. It hurt—and that weekend I would have a bruise on my shoulder.

I darted forward quickly and, with both hands, pushed back against his shoulders with everything I had. He yelped with surprise, staggering backward three paces before he fell over a bunch of kids sitting behind him.

Dillworth went down. The kids went down. The chairs went down. I felt good, even if only for a moment.

One of the kids he tumbled into was Preston. He actually got up before Dillworth did, and was standing behind him when he did get up. I expected Preston to pull something out of thin air. What, I don't know. A Vulcan neck pinch? A lightsaber? What he did was nothing. He just backed away.

Dillworth was up in a blink and tearing towards me. He bounded up to me, dancing on the balls of his feet, and threw the first punch.

I stepped back. He missed, though I could feel the rush of air as his fist raced past my face.

That made him even madder. He rammed into me and then we were both tussling on the cafeteria table. I could feel him pressing against me and the heat of his body was tremendous. He kept mumbling *faggot* under his breath while trying to get a punch in. I had my hands on his shirt collar and school tie, holding him too close to let him hurt me while trying to headbutt him.

The next thing I knew, *my* collar was grabbed from behind. I was pulled off Dillworth and suddenly I was staring into the face of Sister Terrible Smell. Though an old lady, she took Dillworth by the ear like he was a snarling puppy and kept us both at arm's length.

"Stop it!" she screamed.

"He started it!" Not original, I know, but the only thing I could think of saying.

Dillworth, craftier than me, said nothing.

"I don't care who started it," she said, "I'm ending it. Now. Principal's office. March!"

The sister pulled both of us out of the cafeteria, me by the collar and Dillworth by the ear, the room deadly silent in our wake.

Dillworth and I were sitting in the anteroom outside the principal's office. I couldn't help it. My face was red and I was fighting back tears. Nine years in the same school—

counting kindergarten—and never in trouble once till now. Dillworth, an old hand at school discipline, just looked at me with contempt.

The worst part of it, I hated him and also thought he was kinda handsome. For a punk.

The principal's door opened and I saw Sister Ruth, the principal, sitting at her desk with Sister Terrible Smell standing before it.

"Mr. Dillworth," Sister Ruth said. Dillworth rose with sullen dignity and entered the sanctum. The door closed ominously.

I wondered if they were going to eat him.

A few minutes later Dillworth left, red-faced as I was, and passed me without a word. From inside I hear, "Mr. Wilcox."

I swallow and walk to my fate.

To my surprise, it wasn't that bad. Sister Ruth was always mostly okay (as principals go) and mostly told me how disappointed she was in me. I was always "such a nice boy" and she was shocked to see me here for fighting. Especially, she said, after my mother told her how much I wanted to be a priest.

I pricked up at that one. *I* wanted? Wisely, since I seemed to be getting off light, I figured I had better keep my mouth shut. For a change, if nothing else.

When I was released with a reminder to be the "young, upstanding Catholic gentleman" I was meant to be, I slipped out of the office. Sister Terrible Smell brought up the rear.

When the principal's door closed, Sister Terrible Smell took me again from behind by the collar. I turned around, waiting for the smack I knew that was coming.

Instead, she looked at me with concern as her grip loosened. Then, without warning, she said, "Next time someone throws a punch, duck. Don't lean back. They can still get you. And if you duck, you can always headbutt them on the way up."

And without another word, she left.

That's the thing about Sister Terrible Smell—make that Sister Thereselle—and every other grownup. You just never know what they're thinking.

I was hoping that Sister Ruth wouldn't call home and I came in after school with my face scrunched up, expecting the worst. Nothing. Instead, Mom asked, "How was school?" and I just shrugged before going to my room.

I called A.J., still sick in bed, to tell him I was in a fight. He answered and before I could even say hello, he said, "Preston told me everything."

Of course, I didn't know what Preston considered *everything*, so I told it myself. I left out Dillworth calling me *faggot*. I don't know why. I just did.

A.J. made all the right sounds. Meaning, I think he was impressed. I hung up for homework and dinner, and told him I'd see him later that night.

That night we were having dinner and the television was on in the den so dad could hear the news. He was stuck for a cartoon, he said, and hoped something would "tickle" him while he was eating.

It was chicken, I remember that. Mash and string beans. Funny the things you remember, right? At any rate, I remember reaching for the potatoes and my shoulder killing me thanks to Robert. I winced in pain and Mom noticed.

"You hurt?" she looked up from dinner, concerned.

"Just reached funny," I said, taking the potatoes with the other hand. I scooped some onto my plate and Nancy reached over with her fork and helped herself to some of mine. I was too tired to fight with her.

The news story changed and we could hear something about new data suggesting that same sex marriage increased the statewide number of marriages by something like five percent.

And Nancy asks, "Is Thom going to marry A.J.?"

Suddenly, we were all looking at one another.

I felt my face burn as it grew red.

"We're just friends!" I yelled.

Faggot, Robert Dillworth said.

My mother just smiled at Nancy. "I don't think so, honey."

I ate in silence. I wonder if anyone noticed.

After dinner, I went up and finished my homework. I wasn't in the mood for my PlayStation, so I was just watching reruns of the old, old *Star Trek* when my dad knocked on the door.

"Can I come in?"

I thought it was a stupid question, because he came in to ask it. But who am I to point out the obvious?

"Sure," I said. I didn't turn the set off.

"Just came in to say goodnight."

He never did that.

"Goodnight," said I.

"Everything all right?"

"Sure," I said. Spock was telling Kirk something, but I don't think he was listening either.

My dad nodded and left.

I waited till pretty late before going to A.J.'s room. I fell asleep for a bit and woke up well after eleven o'clock. I figured it was too late and peeled off my clothes and was standing there in my underwear when I looked out the window and saw his light on.

Well, dammit, I thought. *I was in a fight and I want to brag.*

I slid my window open and stepped out into the elm. The branches were coated with a thin layer of ice, and I never felt like I had a secure foothold. My first fight would be my last if I slipped and broke my neck.

I was able to keep my balance holding onto the overhead branches, though I slipped badly near the trunk and spent half a minute holding on for dear life. Then I paced across to the other side like a scared cat.

I saw A.J. under the covers with a laptop open in front of him. I eased up his window and he looked up at the blast of cold air.

I stepped into his room and stood proud, every inch a Jedi knight.

"I've been waiting for you, Obi-Wan," I said, making my voice as deep as it would go. "We meet again at last. The circle is now complete. When I left you I was but the learner. Now, *I* am the master!"

He looked at me, brown eyes steely. "Only a master of evil, Darth!"

Now, A.J.'s mom had been fixing up the house and I noticed what looked like curtain rods in the corner, next to where I was standing. They were the type where one slid into the other. I pulled them apart, as if I was unsheathing a sword, and threw one at A.J.

He didn't even blink. He was out of bed in a second, and he was only in his underwear, like me (I bet he was warmer

32

after my tree-hop, but that's another story). He took his curtain rod and approached.

We had a lightsaber duel with curtain rods, bending them more than a bit as we whacked at one another. I made *vvrrroooommmm* noises with each swipe of my blade. A.J. made this choking noise that sounded like static electricity whenever they connected.

Finally, our curtain rod lightsabers locked, and so did our eyes.

"Your powers are weak, old man," I said, voice deep.

He grinned at me, eyes twinkling. "You cannot win, Darth. If you strike me down, I shall become more powerful than you can possibly imagine."

That was it. I pivoted and swiped and he blocked and thrusted.

The thing is, when you're being stupid, you forget how *loud* stupid can be. It was after eleven at night, the house was asleep, and we were thumping around in our underwear, hitting each other with curtain rods and doing sound effects. A.J. had thwacked my hand with his curtain rod lightsaber and when I dropped it, I grabbed his wrists and tried to get his sword from him. We were thrashing around when the door opened.

It was Mr. Lopez. And he did not look happy.

We stopped what we were doing and stood there in our underwear, looking guilty.

"What are you doing?"

"Playing *Star Wars*," I said. Ever helpful, I thought.

"How did you get into the house?"

A.J. opened his mouth to say something, but since I felt like an invincible Jedi knight—and because sometimes I'm dumber than dog dirt—I said, "I climbed across the tree to the window."

From the look on his face, I thought at any moment blood would come gushing out of Mr. Lopez's nose. After he made a gurgling sound he only said, "You, go home."

I looked around for a place to put my lightsaber. Seeing none, I just sort of dropped it on the floor. It made a really final *clank* noise.

Mr. Lopez pointed at A.J. "And we'll talk in the morning."

Mr. Lopez walked me to the front door as if I was a convict or something. It felt strange to be walking around his house in my underwear, but then I thought, *now you think of that.* A.J.'s sister, Lupe, was visiting that week and she saw me being marched through the corridor in my briefs. I don't know what she was thinking, but she didn't say anything.

Without a word he ushered me to the other side of the front door and shut it behind me. I padded through the icy lawn in my bare feet and made it to my door.

Dad didn't lock the door until he went to bed himself. Sometimes he drew until late in the night, then took a walk before climbing into bed. If he was awake, the door was open. But then, he might see me come in. If he was asleep, I'd have to ring the bell. And then I'd be dead.

Freezing, I reached for the doorknob.

Open!

I pushed the door in as quietly as possible and closed it softly behind me. I heard the handle *click* and held my breath, hoping it didn't make too much noise.

I looked around. Nothing.

I took a breath.

I turned and started for the stairs.

"This had better be good."

I froze in my tracks. Slowly I turned and saw dad standing at the door of the kitchen. He had a cup of coffee in one hand, and a pen in the other.

I stood there in my underwear. My mouth was working, but no sound came out.

He sighed. A sound that came from deep within his cardigan sweater.

"Later," he said.

I raced up the stairs and closed my door.

***

The next day, I thought I had got off scot-free (By the way, who is Scot, and would anyone pay for him, anyway?). But I would be wrong once again.

I came down to breakfast. It was Saturday and Nancy was still at the kitchen table. I can eat three days' worth of food and assorted snacks in the same time it takes her to eat one lousy bowl of cereal, but that's a topic for another time. I made myself a bowl of cereal and sat next to her and started eating.

My mother came in and poured herself another cup of coffee. Aside from a smooch on the top of my head, nothing,

My dad followed, also with an empty cup. He said hello. I continued eating.

Yes! I thought. *Nothing. That was close.*

Then the phone rang. We all had cells, of course, but we also had a house phone in the kitchen. My dad picked it up, listened, and then said, "Hi, Fernando."

I started eating faster.

I saw my dad looking at me as he listened. I quickly finished and rinsed out my cereal bowl. I was heading straight for the door when he put his hand over the receiver and said, "Wait."

I did.

My dad finally said, "I'll talk to him." Pause. "Okay. Say hello to Lourdes. Bye."

He hung up and looked at me. Before he could open his mouth, the phone rang again.

"Hello?" he said. "Oh, Sister Ruth."

That's it. I might as well have gone upstairs and packed. I wondered if there was any way I could get to Alaska. There may have been opportunities for a *Star Wars* fan in the frozen tundra.

My father looked at me, eyes pained. "Yes, I understand," he said.

I pointed at myself, as if to ask, *is this about me?* Stupid, I know. But I didn't have anything else.

My father nodded with a snarky smile. If this was a game, he had just sunk my battleship. "Yes, Sister Ruth, I'll talk to him." My father looked at me as he nodded again into the phone. "Yes, I will. Thank you for calling."

He hung up, never taking his eyes off me.

"What is it?" my mother asked.

"It seems your son here, young Father Wilcox, was fighting in school," my father said. It was almost as if he was laughing at me rather than mad. "America's Boy Priest was mixing it up with some guy in the lunchroom."

I never knew when he was teasing me or teasing mom. Sometimes, when he was at the top of his game, he could be doing both at the same time.

"Thomas!" my mother shouted. She turned to dad. "With who?"

"Some kid," my dad said, "Robert Dillweed."

Dillweed? Did Sister Ruth call him that? Sister Thereselle? Or was he making his own little joke? My dad sure liked his own little joke.

"Thomas, how could you?" my mother asked.

I was going to say, *it was easy*, but decided against it. I didn't know what Sister Thereselle told Sister Ruth, and I didn't know what Sister Ruth told dad, so I decided to cough up some version of the truth. I told them the whole story, except for the part about Dillworth calling me *faggot*. That embarrassed me. I felt my face growing red. Not because I felt guilty. That *faggot* really bothered me.

My mother folded her arms. "What does Sister Ruth want us to do?"

My dad shrugged. "Nothing. She just wanted us to know." He turned to me. "You know that behavior isn't acceptable. Right?"

I nodded.

"All right, it's over," he said.

I let out a sigh of relief. I said, "I'm sorry," and turned to go back to my room.

"What did Fernando want?" my mother asked.

I froze. I was getting a lot of practice at freezing that morning.

"Oh, nothing," my dad said.

Nothing?

"More coffee?" my mom asked.

"In a minute," I heard my dad say. I was already climbing up the stairs when I saw that he was behind me. I kept going, hoping he was heading to their bedroom, but he followed me into my room and closed the door.

I said nothing. My new default.

Without a word, my dad went to my bedroom window and slid it open. He reached down and grabbed hold of the branch I walked on. He pulled on it a moment, then scanned the upper branches where I grabbed hold. He then looked down at the lawn below and whistled.

He closed the window. "A guy falling from that tree could get hurt."

"Yes." Not original, but the best I had at that moment.

"You know why Mr. Lopez called?"

"Yes." My second new default.

"Thom," he said, sitting on the window sill, "We always let you guys have sleepovers whenever you want."

"I know."

"So why this?"

I shrugged. "It's not for sleeping over. It's just when I want to tell him something, or we need to hang out."

He looked at me and I wondered if he was going to put me on eBay.

"Do me a favor," he said.

"What?"

"Don't get killed."

With that, he walked to the door. "And don't piss off Fernando any more than you have to. It makes it harder on A.J. Clear on that?"

"Yes." I paused. "Dad?"

"Yes?"

"It's Dillworth. Not Dillweed."

"You don't say?"

He left.

I never really knew how to react to things like that. I expected to have my butt handed to me. I *deserved* to have my butt handed to me. Instead, he was nice. I have a great dad. That doesn't mean I understand him. Not for a minute.

Later that day, A.J. was feeling better and we were tearing around the park. I was going to pick him up at his place, but he texted me to meet him at the park. So I did.

The park near our house is great. It's got a large expanse of lawn that supports three full baseball diamonds. Not that we played. We thought baseball was for dorks, but that was going to quickly change. Except for the playing part (I'll explain later. It's complicated).

There are also swings, not that I used them anymore (I *lived* on them at one time), a wading thingy for real little kids that sprinkles water when it's hot, and tons of trees.

A.J. and I always made for the trees. I remember reading in a book that *great men always return to the trees* (I think it's *The Once and Future King*, but don't make me swear to it). Whenever me and A.J. go to the trees, I quote that. *Great men* includes him. I think that's awfully big of me.

We were big on climbing trees, even in that last year of grade school. I caught up to him on the bicycle path and we made for our favorite tree and climbed. I settled on a branch and asked, "You get in trouble?"

"Yes."

"Bad?"

He shrugged. "You?"

"He didn't kill me," I said. "He also told me not to go out of my way to piss off your dad."

"Sounds smart."

We were both silent, pondering our shared wisdom.

Then, "What do you want to do?"

"Let's walk around," he said.

There are a lot of ways I could close out the story of our last year at St. Benedict's, but I think what happened this day would make the best job of it. There were still several more months of school, and we both knew we were going to St. John's Academy, an all-boys school a couple of miles away. We also knew that our grades were pretty good, and we wouldn't have any trouble making the transition. Also, a lot of the guys from St. Benedict's were going to St. John's, so we wouldn't be hurting for any friends Not that A.J. ever hurt for friends. Everyone always liked him. Most of my friends liked me because A.J. liked me. If I was good enough for him, I was good enough for them.

But I think I'll close grade school with this day because two things happened that really planted the seed for the next couple of years.

First, was baseball. When we left the trees we nosed around the baseball fields. We had seen baseball games before and never really cared. Never played, either. But today, A.J. stopped us in our tracks and just stared.

It was the St. Benedict's team playing the Catholic school from the next town. We didn't know the inning, or the score, or even how well our team was doing. But A.J. stood rooted like one of our trees, eyes filled with the game.

He climbed into the bleachers and watched the rest of it. I looked at him looking at the game, then turned my attention to the game. I was not impressed. I turned to him again, but, suddenly, I ceased to exist.

I never knew what it was that grabbed A.J that day, but he was grabbed. Over the next couple of weeks I would catch him at his place watching baseball, and sometimes he would even talk with the other kids at school about the games he saw on TV. I didn't get it. But his interest in *Star Wars* was turned off almost overnight. Go figure.

We watched until the end and then I watched A.J. as he watched the players shake hands and then trek off into the distance.

"Well," I said. "That was dull."

"I don't know," A.J. said, still looking at the players.

"Let's go home," I said. I felt…I don't know. Jealous. I guess.

What happened next could be called the Second Big Thing That Happened That Day.

We left and went to my place. As I came in, Mom said, "Preston's here. I told him to hang out in your room."

Mothers do that. I don't like people in my room when I'm not there, but moms think you're cool with it. I told her lots of times I'm not, but didn't get anywhere with her on that.

"You're not hiding anything," she said, once. My mother thinks privacy is some kind of mental disorder. Maybe girls think privacy is some kind of mental disorder only when men practice it. I don't know. I'll get back to you on that.

At any rate, I let it drop. I wasn't going to win that one.

If someone was going to be hanging around my room without me, I couldn't hope for better than Preston. He doesn't have to paw through all of my private stuff. He just looks through things with those X-ray eyes and *knows*. He would spook Spock.

We came in and Preston was sitting on the floor, his back against my bed, nose in an oversized book. It wasn't one of mine, so he must've brought it with him.

"Hey," A.J. said. It's things like that which make me think I'm the better talker.

"Hello," Preston said. He didn't look up from his book.

"Thanks for helping me with Dillweed." It is all I could muster at the moment.

"You didn't need my help," Preston said.

"Oh, no?"

Preston looked up. "If you didn't stand up to Dillworth he was going to make your life miserable for the rest of the year," he said. "You're too smart to put up with that. I had faith in you."

That's Preston. He can make turning his back on you sound like a growth experience. Oddly enough, I thought he was right, so I kept my mouth shut.

"What are you reading?" A.J. asked, sitting on my desk.

"*Lord of the Rings.*"

"Gag." That was my contribution.

"Ever read it?" Preston again.

"My mom wants me to, but it'll never be a hobbit with me." That was me. I liked that one.

Preston closed the book and tossed it over his shoulder onto my bed. It landed with a thud. "I'll leave this one here. I have another at home."

"You always buy two copies?"

"Only of the important ones," he said.

"I'm not reading it."

"Why?"

"Elves, gnomes and hobbits," I said. I raised an eyebrow. That's usually effective.

He just nodded, his natural frown more pronounced than ever.

And that was it. In one day, I was introduced to baseball and hobbits—the two things that would obsess both me and A.J. for the next couple of years.

We had graduated to Upper Nerddom.

Chapter Three

So, we went to high school.

I should say upfront that I mostly liked my time at St. John's Academy. On the plus side, it's an all-boys school. That was good because we didn't have to do a lot of grandstanding in front of girls to look cool. You could pretty much just be yourself at St. John's. Within limits.

There were groups that you could fall into but they all had these weird places where they would intersect. Lots of the jocks were also nerds, so the baseball guys would hang with the science fiction guys. Or the religious guys—that's where my mom wanted me to be—would also be at the top of track and field. And the brainiacs could do all the student government stuff they wanted because...well, honestly, because the rest of us didn't really care.

St. John's wasn't far from St. Benedict's, and we could get the bus or, sometimes, one of our mothers would drive us. A.J.'s mom was usually at work on translation before school started, so more often than not my mom would take us. My dad, glued to the news for an idea for a cartoon, was also on hand. But both A.J. and I thought he was such a lousy driver that it wasn't worth it. If your dad drives like mine, here's a word to the wise: take the bus.

I didn't cry my first day at St. John's, so no need for A.J. to hold my hand. In hindsight, I almost kinda wish I did.

A.J. wasn't the only carryover from St. Benedict's. Preston went there, too. As with everything, he had this eerie calm that made me feel as if the world could not touch him. He entered the gym for orientation the first day with that silent mastery you see when Spock beams down to some galactic backwater. I'm not even sure he was always paying attention to his surroundings.

And, yes, Dillworth too—and, if anything, we hated each other now more than ever. It's not like we ever fought again, or that he even tried to ambush me with some knuckles to the forehead. But he would look at me with open hatred, and I would try to top him by sneering at him with disdain. You know. Like Republicans and Democrats.

That first day I was a lot like Preston—I also only had one foot in reality. After he had left *The Lord of the Rings* in my room months before, I did my best to studiously avoid it. I spent most of my time reading Arthur C. Clarke (go find him), Ray Bradbury (ditto, ditto) and *Dune* (I blow hot and cold on that). I also read a lot of *Star Wars* novels, especially the ones about Han Solo. On my best days, I liked to imagine that there was a little Han Solo type swagger in me. Then I'd think about it and figure I wasn't even as cool as C-3PO.

But back to the *Rings*. The book was huge…and I just didn't want to make that kind of time investment. I had started keeping a list of all the books that I had read in the course of a year, and I was afraid that I would invest 500 pages into that thing and give it up, losing lots of reading time and hurting my final number of books read. Before you think this too crazy, I also kept lists of all the movies I saw in a year, and all the games I won. No wonder Preston liked me.

It was my mom, of all people, who changed this.

She was in my room, which always makes me nuts. I was just coming home from school and I found her in my room when I got upstairs "just tidying up".

"Mom, I asked you not to do that."

"You're not hiding anything?" she asked again, all innocent. Remember what I said before about mothers and privacy. Oh well. I bit my tongue and put my books on my desk.

"You reading this?" she asked, holding up *Rings*.

"Thinking about it."

"Why haven't you started?"

"It's too long," I said. "I'm afraid I won't get into it."

"Wait here," she said, putting the book on my bed (Where did she think I would go?). In a few minutes, she returned with a paperback. "Here."

I took the book. "What is it?"

"*The Hobbit*," she said. "It's sort of the book that starts the whole *Rings* trilogy. Read that one. If you like it, you can move onto the *Rings*."

"Why are you always pressing hobbits on me?"

"Ah," she said, moving to the door. "We'll talk about that after you finish it."

That seemed a little sinister to me at the time, and I held off from *The Hobbit* almost as long as I held off from *The Rings*. But one night during my last April in grade school, I had just finished *Fahrenheit 451* for the third time when I looked around for something new.

The Hobbit was there, on a shelf over my desk with a whole bunch of other books I hadn't read, so I took it.

I was hooked. I sat up in bed most of the night reading *The Hobbit*, and came down to breakfast all bleary-eyed the next morning. I told my mom it was her fault I was tired, but she just smiled in that knowing way that moms have (It can be pretty annoying).

I gobbled the book over the next two days, talking to Preston about it a lot. I think the stuff that I liked the most was the stuff at the beginning about Bilbo Baggins' home and his community, the Shire. It seemed a lot like my room.

49

It was comfortable, it was in a place where most people were my friends, and there was a well-stocked kitchen nearby. If I had hairy feet, I'd be a hobbit. Maybe A.J. was more than half-hobbit already; the only place he didn't grow hair was on the bridge of his nose.

I also loved the battles and the dragon and the whole sense that this was a real place that existed a long time ago before we ruined everything with our cement and machines and noise. And it was a place that was a lot more appealing to me than Stony Brook, Long Island.

I passed it on to A.J. as soon as I was done and he read it even faster than I did. The two of us spent a lot of time talking about it with Preston, who, of course, had a theory that the dragon Smaug was a dinosaur who had somehow escaped extinction. You know, even though he turned us onto Middle-earth, I think A.J. and I lived in it while Preston was just a day-tripper.

I think that's why A.J. and I laughed so much more than Preston. It's like this. If someone tells you a joke, you listen to the first part (The setup). And you take the setup in good faith. Then you listen to the second part (The punch line, if you do it right). Then you laugh. But if you question the setup too much, or try to poke holes in it, you never get the joke.

Preston loved *The Hobbit* as much as we did, but he wanted to take it apart and figure it out, like a kid who ruins watches. We just wanted to enjoy it.

My mother didn't miss a chance and told me to get into *Rings* while I remembered everything from *The Hobbit*. I really didn't have to because I'd never forget Bilbo and Middle Earth, but I'm glad I did. *The Lord of the Rings* moved the story on to Frodo, Bilbo's nephew, and his efforts to hike across the vast expanse of Middle Earth—battling wizards and monsters—to destroy the ring. I loved it. When I finished it, I opened it at the beginning and started again.

A.J. couldn't get enough, either. We spent a lot of time talking about what it all *meant*. We were sure it meant something, but we weren't sure what. For a lot of kids, especially smart ones looking to find some kind of argument that holds the whole world together, *Lord of the Rings* looks like it might have some kind of insight into what it all means. And it does. It just took my mother—of all people—to help me figure it out. But more on that later.

A.J. and I also argued over the *Rings* a lot, but that was part of the fun. He thought elves looked like Vulcans. I thought that they were maybe more furry and inhuman. Like the Grinch, but with pointed ears. And if dwarves were small, how much bigger could they be than hobbits, who were only two-to-three feet tall? And what did a hobbit look like, anyway? Again, A.J. thought they just looked like really short guys with abnormally big (and hairy) feet. But that seemed too human to me. I imagined something like gigantic chipmunks who walked on their hind legs and smoked pipes. Or something.

Let me tell you, stuff like this can eat up a whole year of school time.

It was our last June in St. Benedict's that Preston showed up with a piece of paper covered with markings he carefully etched out in magic marker. Both A.J. and I recognized them right away, but I'm the resident big mouth, so I spoke first. "Elvish!" I said. Sherlock Holmes had nothing on me.

"Yes," Preston said, smoothing the paper over the lunchroom table. "Along with a letter key. If you learn this, you can learn to write Elvish."

"Can it teach me to sing?"

"Sing?"

"You know," I said. "Like Elvish Presley."

Preston said nothing. Like I said. No sense of humor.

"If it's so easy, how come you can't do it?" A.J. asked. It's the kind of thing I'd ask, right before opening my mouth and inserting my foot.

Preston refolded the paper and slid it across the table. He opened his spiral notebook and penned a series of runes. He then pushed the book towards me.

I took his letter key for Elvish runes and translated: *Thom isn't funny.*

Well, he gets marks for knowing his stuff.

In just a few weeks, we were writing notes to each other in Elvish. Preston even kept his English lit notes in Elvish, but neither A.J. nor I could write it out that fast. There were also all kinds of rules that went with Elvish that A.J. and I mostly ignored. We enjoyed the pained looks on Preston's face when he read our Elvish notes. He said we "murdered it".

So—to go back to that first day of high school—Preston was mentally somewhere in outer space and I was in the mists of Mirkwood (the eastern region of Rhovanion between the Grey Mountains and Gondor), with Frodo and his bestie, Samwise. I think the only one who was fully awake was A.J.

We didn't have to wear uniforms in high school, like St. Benedict's, but we did have to wear slacks and dress shoes and ties. We could wear sports coats, but most everyone wore a school sweater instead. This was a cardigan, like my dad's, white with red trim. If you belonged to any school clubs or won any sports competitions, you could get a letter and have it sewn onto your sweater. By senior year there were some guys whose sweater was all patches and no sweater.

St. John's was staffed by Christian Brothers. These guys weren't priests, but they were a religious order of teachers. They wore black pants and shirts with clerical collars. There was also a batch of regular teachers, along with several coaches. St. John's was big in track and field, gymnastics, basketball and baseball.

It was this last that got A.J.'s attention. There was a park next to the school, complete with a full-size baseball diamond. A.J. had been making noises about baseball all during our last year at St. Benedict's, but never seemed to do anything about it. Other than watching it on TV. And making me watch it, too. And not caring that I was bored. But no matter.

I was sitting there on the first day, making notes in Elvish and looking at A.J. light up like a Christmas tree at the thought of a baseball team. Preston said nothing. I think he was trying to mind meld with the assistant principal, but I could be wrong.

The three of us (and Dillworth—talk about luck!) all ended up in the same homeroom. It was taught by one of the Brothers, who did his best to dupe us into believing that high school was very grown up and that we would have to act like adults.

Clearly he doesn't know us, Preston wrote in Elvish in my notebook, in a rare attempt at humor.

But it all went fine that first year. A.J. wanted me to go in for baseball, but my heart wasn't in it. He would play during the season and I would go watch the games after school. I went out for track and field, which was something of a mistake. I was always built like a tree trunk, and I was not light on my feet. But I had endurance to spare and could outlast each and every other kid on the team. We'd start a long distance run and I'd lumber along, behind everyone, but everyone else would be out of it while I was still chugging along.

Our grades and specialties pretty much remained the same. A.J. was a math fiend, and he was also the only kid who got a letter for science that year. I got one in English, and also got one for being the head of our religion club. The Liturgical Society. I joined because my mom pushed me to, but I think Preston pointed out the real reason. As head of the club, I got to speak at Mass every week, and Preston says I'm a ham. He's too smart for me to argue with him.

A.J. was no different in high school than he was at St. Benedict's. He was very popular, and being his friend made me popular. At least, while A.J. was around.

The thing about high school is that, when you're there, it's your whole life. When you're in class, that's the most important thing in the world. If you're doing a sport, that's the most important thing in the world. If you're in a club, that's the most important thing in the world (Get my drift?). If you have friends, they're the most important thing in the world.

So, doing all of this stuff takes up all of your time and eats up all of your brain space. I think that school work and baseball would've swallowed up A.J. completely if we didn't have our nerd releases. And I spent so much time doing track (and when I wasn't doing track, I was thinking about it), that *Lord of the Rings* really helped us. It was a separate world we could both go to when the real one was too much.

Not that life didn't have a nasty way of interfering with the best laid plans of mice and hobbits.

I was sitting in the bleachers the spring of my freshman year watching A.J. play ball. I had run four miles with the track team after school, and I sat out there in my gym shorts and sneakers, doodling in my notebook while A.J. played.

I was still drawing. My dad thought I was pretty good, and, frankly, I think he was right. I wasn't going to put Rembrandt out of work, but I could hold a pen with the best of them.

I was sketching goofy stuff and looking at the game. I drew lots of dragons back then, and more than enough elves (Yeah, they looked like the Grinch). I would also doodle stuff in Elvish without thinking. I always thought if I lost my notebook that whoever found it would think it came from another world. That suited me fine.

A.J. was a first baseman and, because of his size and strength, was really good at it. He thought that first basemen were the pack horses of the game, and did all the hard work that made winning possible. I never paid enough attention to professional baseball to see if he was right. But he probably was.

Sometimes he would go to bat, and that was also one of his strengths. He rarely struck out and he was a good hitter, though no superstar. That day, though, we were down three points and it was the bottom of the ninth. The bases were loaded and A.J. came up to bat. He could lose it for St. John's, or win it. I was watching closely.

I would love to say that it was this big, dramatic thing, but it wasn't. He stepped up to the plate and on the first pitch he hit a homer and the ball disappeared into the distance.

The team went crazy. I never saw anything like it. They ran out of the bleachers and started hugging A.J. Then they went really nuts and picked him up, carrying him around on their shoulders.

All right, I went a little nuts, too. I stood at the bleachers, jumping up and down like a lunatic and screaming "A.J.! A.J.! A.J.!" like it was a magic spell. He looked over to where I was and waved, smiling. I felt like I was in outer space.

While I was waiting for everything to finish up, I went back to my notebook and doodled more, and drew a quick picture of A.J. in his baseball uniform, surrounded by Elvish runes. In a little while, A.J. came out of the dugout with his duffle bag and we headed home.

We walked to the bus stop—neither of our moms could pick us up after practice—me going a mile a minute about how great he was. While we were waiting for the bus, Dillworth walked by and casually gave us the finger. No reason. Just for practice, I think. We smiled and waved at him.

When the bus finally came, I kept on about how he blew all the other players out of the water, but A.J. wasn't having any of it. He just smiled indulgently, said that they all "played a good game," and asked if I had made any headway in the trig assignment.

But that's A.J.

We went over the trig problems, which also made me admire him a little more that day. For me, looking at math was like looking at Elvish runes to other people—weird marks on the paper that didn't mean anything. A.J. helped me decipher all of this and pointed me in the right direction to get it all done by tomorrow.

We got off the bus and went to our houses. He gave me a high five when I reached my door and I told him I'd sneak into his room later and do PlayStation if I could get away.

Inside, Mom asked how track was and I said I was the last man standing. She was impressed (Funny. I didn't tell A.J.). I went up to grab a shower before dinner and she told me that Preston was in my room.

I was going to make a big fuss about that, but dropped it. Again. She was never going to learn, and Preston wasn't a snoop. Good thing I don't have too many friends coming over.

I opened my door and there was Preston, sitting in his usual place on the floor by my bed. His nose was in a book. It was something called *True Grit*, which he told me was a Western. You could never tell with Preston.

"Hey," I said. Not the most original thing, but, c'mon, I just ran four miles.

He mumbled something into the book.

I put my books on my bed. I clearly didn't do a good job of it because they fell beside Preston. My notebook fell open beside him and he looked at the drawings and the Elvish runes.

"You're getting better," he said.

"My dad says that artistic ability runs in the family," I said.

"I meant your Elvish."

"Oh," I sat at my desk and pulled off my sneakers. "You here for a reason or just moving in?"

Preston idly took a red marker from his shirt pocket and started translating some of the Elvish words I had written. "I'm making a study of the mathematically challenged," he said. He was so dry, I never knew when he was joking.

"You came to the right place," I said. At least I told the truth. "I'm going to grab a shower. Want to wait around and have dinner? I'm sure mom won't mind."

"Hmmm…" he said, translating.

"I'm making a study of weirdos with red pens," I said, taking the towel off the hook of my bedroom door. "Back in a minute."

I went and showered (Despite what you may have heard, I shower every week. Whether I need to or not. That's a joke, by the way). I toweled off and brushed my hair then went back to my room with my towel around me.

I went back into my room and Preston was still working through my notebook, translating the Elvish I had scribbled in the margins and on the back cover and, sometimes, on the back of assignment papers.

I pulled on some boxers under my towel, then took it off and grabbed a blue T-shirt. I was looking around for some socks when I thought it might be a good idea to see if Preston was ever going to return to humanity again.

"I heard that they beamed you down to a hostile planet," I said.

He paid no attention.

"Fortunately, your Vulcan blood made you immune to a dangerous parasite."

He just sort of went *hmmmmm* under his breath.

"Too bad the Prime Directive wouldn't let you help any of those planetary screw heads," I said.

Still nothing. Before I could say anything else, though, he capped his pen and put my notebook on the bed. "Getting better," he said.

I had pulled on fresh jeans and went to the bed to page through my notebook.

Now, usually I just doodle in Elvish without thinking about what I'm writing down. I saw that I had written down my own name several times, then my hobbit name (Isembard Goldworthy, if you must know), and stupid stuff, like "math sucks".

I was paging through his translations when I saw something that stopped me dead.

There, near the middle of the book, I had written the same thing maybe ten times, and Preston's translation in red was at the bottom of each line.

Under the Elvish runes, Preston translated: *Thom loves A.J.*

I never realized that I wrote that. Most of my Elvish runes were just top-of-mind stuff. I never even re-read it myself. I felt my face grow hot.

Faggot, Robert Dillworth said

Preston saw my look of shock, but his own face was impassive. I quickly started moving through the other pages.

There was nothing else embarrassing. I said something. I don't know what. I'm sure it sounded like gibberish.

I looked at Preston again.

He shrugged.

A shrug, I wondered. *What the hell does that mean? They're just kids?*

I was going to say something else, but my mouth was all dry.

"I wonder if there was a planetary outbreak of disease," he said, "would the Prime Directive still be applicable. What do you think?"

I gibbered something.

"And it depends on the captain, of course," he added.

I closed the book and sat at my desk. I controlled myself because I thought I was going to cry.

"And on the quadrant," he added. "Though I'm sure the Federation would help the Klingons just as fast as they would help, say, the Metrons. Not that they would need the help."

I had no idea who the Metrons were (and I bet you don't, either), but nodded. I was relieved I didn't have to say anything.

Preston sighed. Interstellar diplomacy was always a trial for him. "You'd think the Guardian of Forever would be of help. But...politics."

He got up and walked to my door. "Can't stay for dinner. Double check your trig. I don't think you got the third problem right. It's the same problem A.J. always has."

A.J.? My ears pricked up. "About A.J.," I started.

Before I could say a word, Preston shrugged. And—did I really (really, *really?*) see this?—I think he *winked* too. "Later," he said.

Before I could follow he was gone. On the bridge of the Enterprise somewhere, I thought.

No matter. I had a lot to do. I'd be called to dinner in a few minutes. I tore the offending pages out of my notebook and ripped them into tiny, tiny pieces. Then I went to my window and threw them into the wind. I watched *Thom loves A.J.* in Elvish blow away into the night sky.

Faggot, Robert Dillworth said

Then I took my notebook and shoved it under my shirt. I walked casually downstairs and through the kitchen.

"Don't go far," Mom said. "Dinner in a few."

I mumbled and went out back. I opened one of the garbage cans and pulled up a plastic bag filled with kitchen gunk. I threw my notebook at the bottom of it, then covered it with garbage.

I didn't say much at dinner. Nancy was talking up a storm and mom and dad asked me about my day, but they didn't get a lot out of me that night. Mom asked if I was okay and put a hand on my forehead. I pulled away.

"He feels warm," she said to dad.

"Maybe you should make an early night of it, son," he said. I knew what he was thinking. *Don't go to A.J.'s place. Did he know...?*

"'Kay," I said.

When it was over I went to my room. I had left the window open by mistake, and though it was spring, the night air was cold. My room was chilled. I closed the window and climbed into bed fully dressed. Staring up at the ceiling.

What did it all mean? I didn't think I would even find the answer in the *Rings*.

I didn't sleep a lot that night. I did know when I finally got out of bed that things would have to change. I would have to act different.

But what that meant, I had no idea.

Chapter Four

So, we became sophomores.

Like all things, it didn't happen at once and the change was gradual.

The fallout from "losing" my notebook lasted a few days, then died down. My mom just groused about my carelessness, my dad said it was a shame to lose all of those good drawings (he never once mentioned the schoolwork), and Preston offered me his notes to copy. And he never said anything about anything else. He *does* make me wonder.

I had decided to *act* different, but I still didn't really know what that meant. I didn't think I *acted* like a guy who would write *Thom loves A.J.* in his notebook, but what would acting like that mean?

At first, I decided not to think about it too much. But then, I thought about not thinking about it too much. If that makes any sense. And then I was thinking about thinking about not thinking about it too much. If this makes you confused, think of how I felt.

At any rate, I can't say I *acted* any differently for the rest of my freshman year. But I *did* think about how to react to everything and anything before I did it. And that was exhausting.

The easiest way around it all was to just concentrate on what I was doing, and *be* that.

So I trained really hard. I was never going to be a track and field superstar – too slow and too solid – but I was a valued member of the team thanks to my endurance and desire to compete. And because I won the school several medals, I don't think anyone was going to care too much about what I wrote in Elvish. Or so I hoped.

The other thing was that my baseball connection to A.J. changed completely. In a word, we were *spiked*.

It happened this way.

During the spring and early summer of our freshman year, we surrendered to a new craze. One that almost wiped out *Star Wars* and *Lord of the Rings*. And that was Jayson Tuttman, the greatest first baseman in the history of the New York Mets. His stats, at that time, were .310/.394/.574, OPS – .969, Hits – 2,749, HRs – 575, RBIs – 1,758. He was a colossus walking among mere mortals, was Jayson Tuttman, and A.J. and I could not get enough.

To those non-baseball nerds out there, a first baseman fields ground balls that are hit in his vicinity and catches throws from other infielders to force a runner out at first base. The first baseman often has to "scoop" one-hop throws from an infielder or pick low throws out of the dirt. And because they are often powerful but not fast, first basemen rank well on baseball's home run and RBI leaderboards.

And it wasn't just that Jayson was the best-of-the-best that year. It was that the fans and the media loved him. It started like this.

That spring, Jayson was on-camera in a post-game interview, answering questions while taking off his cleats. For that reason, the nickname *Spike* came out of that interview, and for the next few years, he was known as Spike. Or the Emperor of First Base. Me, I liked the name Spike. It didn't take so long to say.

He also became a media superstar. The thing was, on top of being great at the game, Spike was really (really) good looking. He was tall and blond with that type of fluffy, thick hair that floats down around his head like a halo. He had clear light-blue eyes that were almost green, and when he smiled, these creases formed in either cheek.

He was also tall and loaded down with muscle. In no time at all, Spike moved from the covers of magazines like *Sports Illustrated* to *People* and *US Weekly*. Everything he said was news (Not that I ever noticed him saying anything interesting). Everywhere he went was news (But they were mostly famous places already, so see the previous parentheses). He also dated lots of famous women (Not that I would know. At this time in my life, most of the famous people I knew of were hobbits or part of the Rebel Alliance). And he played a *great* game of ball. And I mean *great*.

It got so that A.J. would never miss a Mets game, and I would sit with him, usually in his room, watching. I had grown more interested in the game the more I saw of it, and the fascination we shared for all things Spike was another bond.

Spike was more than a great player. Spike was also a great showman. His antics made the game even better. He would make faces at the camera. He would make bogus hand signals. He would yawn loudly between pitches. It was some of the best television of the time.

Sometimes we'd watch at my house with my dad. He thought all this showmanship was unprofessional. That's my dad. The first one to tell a joke, and the last one to think you should do it too. Other times, we'd catch the game in A.J.'s living room, but Mr. Lopez made me nervous. We'd be watching the game, but sometimes I'd catch him watching me. I sometimes felt like he thought I was going to steal the silverware. So we watched mostly in A.J.'s room.

But soon, just watching the game wasn't enough. When Spike was on a talk show, I'd creep over the elm into A.J.'s room and we'd watch before bed. We even DVR-ed some games, just so we could watch them again.

Before you knew it, we were both buying *People* and *US Weekly* just to read about him (A comedown from Tolkien,

I know, but this was a mania). Preston said that if there was a book called *Nothing About Jayson Tuttman*, that *really* had nothing about him in it at all, we'd still buy it. For Preston, it was a rare instance of humor and another example of him being always right.

And then came the poster.

That breakout summer for Jayson Tuttman was also when he was featured on a poster that soon ended up on walls around America.

It was a picture of Jayson, shirtless and wearing his Mets pants and cleats. He had dark grease marks under his eyes to cut down glare, and he looked soulfully into the camera. He held a baseball bat, and the muscles in his chest and arms gleamed with oil. He stood on first base and there were several baseballs at his feet. And there, at the top of the poster in enormous letters, was his name: SPIKE!

Well, that summer between freshman and sophomore year, when it was A.J.'s birthday, I got him that poster as a present. When he opened it at his birthday party he started laughing. I didn't know what he was thinking and when he saw my face he said, "Wait a minute."

He ran upstairs and came down with a long tube gift wrapped. "Here," he said. "I was giving this to you for your birthday."

I opened it up and laughed, too.

It was the same poster.

My poster of Spike ended up over my bed, relegating the poster I had of *Star Wars: The Force Awakens* to over my desk. I had also gotten a softball and I would throw the ball against the poster, catching it and throwing it for hours on end. Or until my father came into my room and told me to knock it off. Sometimes both.

So we were dedicated Spike-heads for all of our sophomore year. A.J. played lots of baseball that year, taking ownership of first base, and getting better and better at it. I'd still go to as many games as I could after track and cheer him on.

I sometimes thought that maybe Preston would feel that we weren't friends anymore because he never showed any special interest in baseball. Or in Spike, for that matter. But whenever I mentioned the game or our favorite first baseman, Preston was always able to rattle off the latest scores, Spike's stats, and even celebrity news. Did I mention that I wondered about him?

It was also when we were fifteen that our folks started letting us take the train to the city to sometimes catch the Mets games at Citi Field. It took the better part of two hours to get into New York by train, and then nearly another hour to get into Queens and our seats. But those days were special to us.

Mr. Lopez was very unhappy about our going to the games at first. I don't know why he finally changed his mind. Because it was baseball? Because we were outside? Who knows? I never did find out what A.J.'s punishment was for us using the tree to get into each other's rooms. A.J. never told me, but we never stopped traveling that way, either.

Sometimes parents blow up about things and then turn a blind eye to them. I wouldn't be surprised if my dad called him after talking to me. Either way, we weren't complaining.

We'd usually go during the weekend (on weekdays, we'd come home too late at night, my mother said). We'd take lunch with us and make a day of it. A.J. got the printed Yearbook and it became his holy book. We'd both page through it before the game, reading and rereading the same words until I could almost recite them by heart.

Of course the Mets knew that Spike was now the main draw, and featured him in all of their marketing. Spike Fever had gripped the fans, and we were surrounded by guys holding up banners with his name. Some guys even showed up in cleats with his name painted on them.

One good thing about being crazy is that moment when you realize you're not alone.

My sophomore notebook had nothing in Elvish, but it *was* covered with my usual doodles, drawings and sketches. Now my notebook was full of sketches of Spike. This was actually a good thing in many ways. Before, most of my sketches were cartoony. You know. Big feet, oversize hands, faces that were more suggested than drawn. But Spike was such a perfectly proportioned athlete that just drawing him again and again made me a better artist.

Surprisingly, even though they looked nothing alike, A.J. was a lot like Spike. Both were very tall, with long torsos and powerful arms and legs. I once told A.J. this before a game and I think he stood ten feet taller on first base that day.

Thanks to *People*, we knew where Spike liked to hang out and on those weekend trips to New York, we would hang around them too, hoping to see him up close. There was a famous bar in lower Manhattan called McSorley's Old Ale House. The first time we went we got thrown out (before we had even walked three feet in) for being too young. That didn't stop us from waiting outside. Early one day, we actually stood outside McSorley's for three hours before a game, hoping Spike would show up. We were about to do this again the next week until I told A.J. it was unlikely that Spike would go to a bar right before a game.

We also got thrown out of the anteroom of the Mets' locker room more times that I can count. There were a couple of times that we caught sight of Spike up close, but various flunkies always pushed us back outside. We yelled at Spike that we were his biggest fans, but I don't think he heard us.

A.J. got the idea that we should send him a fan letter and tell him that we were coming to a certain game and would like to meet him. Since I was the one who was good at English, I said that I'd do it. It went like this:

Dear Spike,

My name is Thom Wilcox and I live in Stony Brook, New York, next door to my best friend, A.J. Lopez.

A.J. and I are your biggest fans. We each have your poster in our room, and read about you in all the magazines.

We are going to be at the game on the last Sunday of the month. We would like to meet you after the game and maybe hang out. Do you do PlayStation, too? We can also talk about Star Wars and Lord of the Rings, if you like that stuff.

My phone number and email are at the bottom of this letter. Feel free to call me when you get a chance. If I don't hear from you, we'll ask at the gate after the game.

Keep winning for us!

Your fans,

Thom Wilcox and A.J. Lopez

We didn't get an answer.

That Sunday we showed up at the gate after the game trying to get into the locker room. Some guy in a Mets jacket started screaming at us.

I explained to him that we wrote Spike a letter.

That…didn't seem to change his mind. He told us to get lost.

On the train, A.J. decided that maybe Spike didn't get the letter, so he would write one himself. And he did. It went like this:

Dear Mr. Tuttman,

I am writing to set an appointment to meet with you and discuss your remarkable baseball career.

I have been following your exploits for several years, and have decided, based on the evidence, and thanks to examining the available video footage provided, that you are the finest first baseman in the league today.

I, too, am a first baseman on my school team. Many people have said that there are similarities between the two of us. I think we would have a great deal to discuss.

I have also been studying the history of the game, and think a mutual pooling of our mutual insight would be mutually beneficial.

My address is on the envelope. Perhaps, if an in-person meeting is not possible, thanks to your schedule and devotion to the game, we could correspond. It would be mutually beneficial.

Many thanks for your consideration in this matter.

I beg to remain, yours,

Mr. Alberto Javiar Lopez, Esq.

Now, I saw multiple problems with this letter. I told A.J. that I think he used "mutually beneficial" too many times. He just shrugged that off.

"When you're dealing with important people like Spike," he said, like he deals with important people like Spike every day, "you have to convince them that what you are offering is...mutually beneficial."

"And how is meeting us beneficial to him?"

He opened his mouth, then closed it before opening it again. "I think my knowledge of the game might give him greater insight."

"What special knowledge do you have," I wondered, "other than being a darn good first baseman yourself?"

He shrugged. "I could study and come up with something."

I went on that I didn't think he could call himself *esquire*. I said, "I don't mean to sound like Preston, but unless I'm mistaken, that means that you're a lawyer."

"No it doesn't," he said, with complete assurance. "It just means that you're a gentleman."

"Are you a gentleman?"

"Well I never hurt nobody."

I nodded. "Well, there's that," I pointed to the closer. "And why do you beg to remain?"

I got him with that one. He seemed puzzled for a moment, and then said, "I took that from a book."

Well, a book was good enough for me. It didn't sound like something you'd find in Middle Earth—but A.J. read more mysteries than I did. I left it in.

So, I rewrote A.J.'s letter on my computer, printed it out and off it went. We waited for two weeks and almost gave up hope until we came home from school one day and found a large manila envelope from the New York Mets addressed to A.J. Lopez.

We rushed upstairs with it eager to start our new friendship with the Emperor of First Base. But when we opened it, we found another copy of the Yearbook that A.J. already had, and a photo of Spike with a pre-printed autograph on it.

It didn't matter, because A.J. was delighted with it, anyway. He had a framed eight-by-ten photo of him and his sister Lupe near his bedroom door. He took this down and switched the photos in the frame, putting Spike in a place of honor.

He and Lupe were stuck in the top drawer of his dresser.

"I don't think she's going to be happy when she sees that," I said.

"Don't worry," he said, smiling and putting an arm around my shoulders. "I'll switch it back when she comes to visit."

You have to admire that level of thinking.

Me, I wasn't completely satisfied with how the whole letter-writing thing worked out. I think two such heart-felt letters should've gotten some kind of personal response. And I figured, the next time we watched Spike hamming it up during a game, that such a great guy would have responded. Maybe he never got the letters? That seemed reasonable enough. I figured that the Mets just opened letters to players so they wouldn't have to be bothered.

But surely he would want to be our friend, if he had a chance to get to know us.

The question was—*how do we get him to know us?*

So, first I started looking up all the Tuttman's in New York that I could find online. His bio said that he was born and raised in New York, and maybe his family had a phone.

I called fifteen Tuttmans on my quest and struck out every time. One guy – an old one from the sound of his voice—said, "No! And if you call again, I'll have the police on you!"

Then I figured that he probably had an email account. I sent emails to various spellings of his first and last names to AOL and GMAIL accounts. Most of those just came back undeliverable, and some came back saying I had the wrong address.

I did see, on the Mets webpage, an email for the managing office. I used that URL with different iterations of Spike's name, but that also came to nothing.

I called the Mets office and asked to speak with him.

"Kid," the voice on the other end said, "he doesn't come to the phone for just anybody."

"But I'm not just anybody," I said, disgruntled. "I'm his biggest fan."

"So is everybody else," he said. Before hanging up.

(By the way, before I was disgruntled, was I gruntled? Just asking.)

The next idea I had was to make a sign that he would be sure to see from the dugout. A.J. got an old sheet from his mom and I got together all the acrylic paint I had. We took the sheet down to A.J.'s basement and tacked it to the wall.

I downloaded a copy of our Spike poster and put it on the wall next to the sheet and made a really good copy of it with a piece of charcoal. I had spent so much time doodling pictures of him in my notebook, that with just a little effort I can get a really good likeness. I may have even made him look *better*.

Then, with all my experience writing in Elvish, I managed to create something in a sort of fake-Gothic text. And before you know it, had a drawing of Spike, under which was written:

WE ARE YOUR BIGGEST FANS!

It took us the better part of three days to paint it. The first problem was that the only sheet that A.J. could find was a green one, and when we were finished painting in Spike's features, it looked like he was seasick. That then took a major overhaul to get it down right. Also, painting yellow for his hair on top of green gave us a result that looked like a mix of rust and barnacles, and we had to paint over it several times. But, like I said, at the end of three days we had it down and it looked good.

It was nearly another two weeks until we were able to get to another game. Of course, the park security made us unroll our banner at the gate so they could examine it. They weren't handling it too gently and I could see A.J. doing a slow burn. Fortunately, they let it go and we were able to roll it up and get it into the stands.

We were high in the bleachers, but sometime around the seventh inning we moved to the first row of our section and unfurled our banner. Spike was on first base, and the jumbo, stadium-wide TV focused on us and the sign. The entire stadium erupted in applause and A.J. and I were flushed with success. This would be our entrée! I could even see Spike look up at the screen and see our banner, then turn and look towards us. I think. He was far away. But the whole stadium was going wild, so what else could it have been?

We sat back down for the last two innings (we won, by the way, thanks to some great playing by Spike). A.J. and I made a great show of slowly folding our banner and we lingered in the stands while the crowd thinned out.

"What are we waiting for?" I asked.

"Just wait," A.J. said. "They'll come to us."

He was right. They did. We waited so long and the stadium was nearly empty when an usher told us, "Scat!"

A.J. pointed at the folded banner. "But, that was our banner."

"Take it with you," the guy said. "We're closing."

So we did. A.J. had us loiter around out front, convinced that Spike would have "his people" come out and find us. If they ever looked, they missed us, as we went unfound.

We tried the banner for the next two games, but never had the jumbo monitor focus on us again. And on the third and last time some fans were yelling "down in front!" to get us out of the way. So...scratch the banner, despite its early success.

We were watching an old movie near the end of our sophomore year and saw someone get a telegram. A deliveryman in a uniform walked up to the hero, said, "Telegram" and the guy took it and opened it.

I asked my dad what that was, and he said it was like a hand-delivered text back in the days before cell phones.

I could almost see a light bulb light up over A.J.'s head.

That night, he climbed through the window with a knapsack holding his laptop slung over his shoulder.

"There was a thing called Western Union," he said, turning on the monitor. "You can give them a message and then they print it out and hand deliver it to the person it's written to."

"And how is that different from a letter?" I asked. Good question, I thought.

"Well," he thought for a moment. "Anyone can open a letter. But a telegram, that can only go to the person it's meant for. Like a text. It goes right to a person's phone. No one else is going to get it. Right?"

I nodded. It sounded logical.

"They don't have Western Union telegrams anymore, but there are still services that will send them out for you. I've been looking it up. You have to keep 'em short, and end every sentence with STOP. That's how you know you got to the end of it. I have one written out."

Here's what he had written:

MR. JAYSON TUTTMAN,
WE ARE YOUR TWO BIGGEST FANS STOP. WE MADE THAT BANNER YOU SAW ON TELEVISION STOP. WE WOULD VERY MUCH LIKE TO MEET YOU STOP. WHEN WOULD BE A GOOD TIME TO GET TOGETHER? STOP.

"Well," I considered. "It says it."

We got on the phone and tried to order it; no wonder A.J. said telegrams are rare. They said they needed Spike's address, and I looked up Citi Field on the laptop, thinking it would be as good an address as any.

I read them the telegram and we went over it three times before it was correct. Then the guy on the other end of the phone said, "And what credit card will you use?"

"Credit card?"

"To pay for the telegram," he said. Pretty insistent, I thought.

I turned to A.J. "We need a credit card to pay for this. Do you have your dad's?"

"No." His eyes seemed bigger than usual. "Do you have *your* dad's?"

"No." I turned back to the phone. "Could you please keep a record of this and we'll call you back tomorrow?"

"Ma'am," the person on the other line said, "I can't *hold* anything. Will you be sending the telegram at this time or not?"

"Not *ma'am*," I corrected, "*Sir*." I hated when people did that.

"Whatever. Can you pay now?"

"No," I said. "I'll call again tomorrow."

A.J. thought the whole telegram idea was dead, but I promised I'd talk to my dad about it tomorrow.

And I did. My dad said it was a bad idea.

"I don't think that will get you what you want," he said that morning when he was having breakfast.

I sighed.

"Thom," he said, sipping coffee. "Just what *do* you want?"

I shrugged. "We think he's great," I said. "We just want to be his friend."

My dad nodded. He did that a lot. Then he said, "You know, just because he plays a great game of ball doesn't mean that he's worthy of being your friend."

"Worthy of being *my* friend?"

"You're pretty terrific, too," he said. "And you don't have to be a great ballplayer for me to notice it."

That's the thing about parents. They never understand.

I think he could tell I wasn't buying it. "Try and think of something else. If you really want to find a way to be friends with Spike, I'm sure something will come up."

And…it did. But not until next year.

Chapter Five

So, we became juniors.

Our sophomore year ended on a high note: the Mets went into the Pennant race. Sadly, they got traduced by the Cardinals. (Isn't that a great word? Traduced? I got it from an old Nero Wolfe mystery that A.J. gave me.)

Before they lost the series, though, I had one more brainstorm.

One night over the summer I had gone through the tree to A.J.s room and we were hanging out, talking about how the World Series was going to shape up. He got up to get something from his closet and when he reached up to the top shelf, my eyes drifted to the Spike poster over his bed. Once again, I thought of how much alike they look.

"You know," I said, not being very original, "there are times that you really look like Spike."

Now, Spike is big and blond with blue eyes, and A.J. is big and dark-haired with brown eyes, but it was more in the way they were put together and carried themselves that I meant it.

"Really?" he asked. It always made him happy when I said that. He took up his baseball bat and imitated the pose from the poster: putting all his weight on his left leg, throwing the right one out a bit, and resting the bat over his shoulder.

"Yeah," I said. "A lot."

I thought for a minute. "You know," I said, "We could always send Spike a picture of you, copying his poster."

"Yeah?"

"Yeah. And he might want to come and see you play in a game, or something."

"That's an idea," he said. A.J. had already gotten into his sleep clothes at this point: a loose T-shirt and some sweats. He pulled out the neck of his T-shirt and looked down at his torso. "I'm a lot hairier, though."

He pulled up his T-shirt and, yes, he was a hairy kid. He had muscular arms like Spike, and the same broad shoulders and well-defined abs. But where Spike was smooth and well-oiled in the poster, A.J. was hard and furry.

"Well," I said. "We could shave it off."

A.J. instantly thought that was a great idea. He left for the bathroom and came back with a damp washcloth, a can of shaving cream and a razor.

"Help me a minute," he said, pulling off his T-shirt.

A.J. tossed the shirt onto his bed and dampened his torso with the washcloth. He then handed me the shaving cream.

"Here," he said. "Put on a lot."

I pressed some shaving cream onto my palm and started to spread it on his torso.

"That's cold!"

"Sorry," I said.

I rubbed the foam over his pecs and then down onto his abs. I was about to wipe the leftover cream onto the washcloth, but he told me to keep it in case he needed more.

A.J. took the razor and started shaving off the hair on his stomach. It made a scratching noise and he wiped the hair and foam onto the washcloth. Shaving left his skin a little red and scratchy, but with his thick, black hair gone, his abs stood out in hard relief.

He did his lower chest, carefully shaving and wiping away the cream and hair, until he handed me the razor.

"Here," he said. "You do the top of my chest so I don't cut myself."

I took the razor in my dry hand and started shaving A.J.'s pecs. He stood super straight, so his chest really pushed forward. I ran the razor over each pec, taking special care with the indentation in the center of his chest. When I was done, I wiped his chest and then my hands with the washcloth.

Suddenly, I didn't feel all that well.

He stood in front of the mirror and posed with the baseball bat, me standing behind him. He looked great, though his chest was a little raw after the shave.

"I can fix that," he said. He took a bottle of rubbing alcohol from his desk and poured some into his palm before using both palms to rub it all over his torso. He winced in pain but didn't say anything. He then held out the bottle and poured some into my hand.

I rubbed my hands together and then rubbed him down with the alcohol. He winced again, but made no noise. I rubbed him until the alcohol evaporated.

"You okay?" he asked.

I backed away and sat on his bed, a little dizzy. "Yeah," I said. "I must've breathed in too much of that stuff."

He sniffed the alcohol, made a face, and closed the bottle. "Sorry," he said, putting it back in his desk drawer

He picked up the bat again and stood in front of his mirror, posing like Spike.

"Pretty good," he said.

"Great," I said.

He came over to me and put a hand on my head, right over my right ear. I could feel the warmth of him through my hair. "You don't look so good," he said.

I pulled back, away from his hand, "Just tired, I guess."

I got up. My legs were wobbly, "I'm headin' home."

"Wait," he said. He picked up his phone from the bed. "Take the picture!"

I grabbed his phone and had him stand right under the poster, holding the exact same pose. I took three or four pictures to make sure I had it; for some I moved the lens closer to get a better shot of his torso. I then texted the pictures to my own phone.

"Got 'em," I said. "I'll think of a letter to send with them tomorrow."

"Later," he said, as I opened the window.

It was never harder to climb through the tree than it was that night. I felt dizzy and a little light-headed. I had to be extra careful with each step because I also found that my breath was coming in short little bursts.

At last I got into my room and closed the window. I brushed my teeth and got into my own sleep clothes and climbed into my bed. Holding my phone.

Before I went to sleep, I looked at the photos I had taken of A.J. He looked...really good.

I turned off my phone and the light and tried to sleep. Somehow, in the dark, I could see the pictures I had taken of A.J. in my mind's eye. It was a wild night, with tons and tons of dreams of Spike and A.J. and then of the both of them and the three of us. When I woke up the next morning, my head hurt with it all.

A.J., getting caught up in the race to the pennant, forgot all about sending Spike a picture. But I never deleted the photos and kept them in my phone.

I was surprised at how often I would look at them. Mostly at night.

**

That summer, we turned sixteen. Our second greatest priority—after the Mets' winning streak—was getting our learner's permit.

St. John's had a driver's ed. program, and that was keyed in with the city so that all that was necessary to get our permit was to pass the road test. Both A.J. and I did really well in the written portions, and our mothers took turns giving us driving lessons.

My mom took us to the local cemetery to practice, saying, "At least you can't kill anybody here."

She would very patiently sit in the passenger seat and A.J. and I would take turns driving through the cemetery. This was the best practice we could've had. The cemetery roads were always empty during the day, the speed limit was low, and it was almost impossible to get into an accident.

A.J.'s mom was more interested in giving us instruction on active roads. That way, she thought, we would get an idea of what real driving was like. She would drive us through Stony Brook, carefully making sure we did not drive into oncoming traffic or turn without signaling. When the time came for us to take our road tests, A.J. and I aced it on the spot.

The two of us and both of our moms all came in the Toyota that A.J.'s mom drove, and there was some debate over who would drive us home from the test. Both A.J. and I wanted to, but, A.J. just smiled and told me, "You take it."

That's what you call a friend.

So, I drove us all home from the Department of Motor Vehicles. It was the highpoint of my summer.

A.J. and I were very proud to have gone through the whole process so smoothly. Of course, leave it to Preston to make us feel like idiots.

Preston did not take driver's ed. with us, and we teased him about that pretty regularly. When we saw him the day after we got our permits, we told him that we could now drive and, "if you're good, maybe we'll take you somewhere".

Preston reached into his back pocket and pulled out his wallet. Inside was his permit.

I would've said something, if I couldn't think of something to say. It was A.J. who was quicker.

"How'd you do that if you didn't take driver's ed.?"

Preston shrugged, putting away his wallet, "I didn't *need* driver's ed."

Some people. I swear.

The Mets going into the pennant race next summer took a lot of the sting out of returning to St. John's for our junior year.

Except for one major incident, junior year was a lot like our sophomore year, but when one of our moms took us to school, they would let one of us drive (Unless it was snowing. Or raining. Or they were tired. Come to think of it, they didn't let us drive too much).

The major incident that I mentioned is that junior year is the year we got...Spiked.

It happened like this.

Nancy really started it. It was late spring, and we only had a couple more months of junior year left. The Mets were not doing all that well, though Spike was still playing a great game and packing the stadium with his antics. A.J. and I were hooked more than ever, sometimes watching with one or both of our dads. Even Preston would come over and read while it was on, though often A.J. would notice that he was looking up from his paperback book most of the time.

At any rate, we were huddled around the television when Nancy came in and found me, A.J. and dad deep in the game. Preston was there too, but, like I said, who knows how deep he was into the game. For all I know, he may have been silently communicating with Starfleet Command.

Nancy sat for a few minutes, and when Spike came on she said, "Oh, he's going to be in Stony Brook in a few days."

"What?" I don't know if it was me or A.J. who asked. Maybe both.

"That guy," she pointed at Spike, as if we were slow on the uptake. "He's coming here for a few days."

"How do you know?" That was me.

"Diane's mom works at Redfern Hotel. She told me."

Now even dad was interested. "Why's he coming?"

"There's some kind of baseball thing," she said, with typical clarity. "And he's staying at the hotel. Next week, I think. He's making a personal appearance."

A.J. and I were sitting at attention. Even Preston looked up from his paperback. Maybe he was just taking a breath.

This was interesting. Though Spike was still at the top of his game, *People* said the Mets were worried about how he spent his time off-field. Spike was often rowdy at bars, or involved in fights with strangers. It never seemed to affect how he played, but it was plain that management wanted him to clean up his act.

They probably also wanted him to improve his image. Neither of us had heard of him making personal appearances, so this was a new one.

"You think Diane's mom can get us in to meet him?"

Nancy bugged her eyes and shrugged, like I just asked, *Want to spend time studying mushrooms and slugs?*

"Your ambitions have an admirable consistency," Preston said. I didn't say anything because I didn't know if that was a good thing or not. He added, "I would urge you not to waste this opportunity."

My dad, smarter (sometimes) than me or A.J., had already opened his laptop. After two minutes of searching, he found it.

"Local baseball fans can meet the Emperor of First Base, Jayson Tuttman," he read, "next Wednesday at a special event celebrating the release of a new Blu-ray documentary on the history of the New York Mets. Starting with the 1960 World's Series win and going all the way to new superstar Jayson 'Spike' Tuttman, the first baseman will sign the first two hundred Blu-rays sold in the lobby of Redfern Hotel. Tickets required, call..." He lowered the laptop.

"Next week?" A.J. asked.

"Can we get tickets?" I asked.

"I'll call in the morning," my dad said.

A.J. and I looked at each other. Maybe, we thought, this was it. Preston just looked at us like a disappointed parent.

As soon as I got home from school the next day, I ran into my dad's study. Without a word he just turned round on his swivel chair, smiled and shook his head.

I threw my arms around him and hugged hard. "Thanks, dad!"

"I got tickets for you, me and A.J."

"I gotta go tell him."

"He probably knows," I said. "I called his dad earlier."

I heard that, but had already turned and was heading to A.J.'s house. His mom opened the door when I rang the bell and I just ran upstairs, saying a quick hello over my shoulder.

A.J. turned when I came in and we both started jumping around like lunatics. Next thing you know, I was chanting "Mets, Mets, Mets, Mets!" while he was yelling "Spike, Spike, Spike, Spike!". What can I say? We were happy.

The day got better when Nancy told us that she spoke to Diane's mom. Spike was coming to Stony Brook Tuesday, the night before the event, and if we were "handy" when he was in the lobby, she would try to get him to say hello to us.

Mom said she would talk to Diane's mom (did moms have some kind of secret club, I wondered?) and "we'll see how that works out".

I don't have to tell you that A.J. and I were crazy the next few days. I would catch myself in my room, looking at my poster of Spike, thinking that in a few days I'd get to meet him. That the hand holding that bat would soon shake *my* hand. It was pretty exciting stuff.

It all turned out to be a catastrophe.

My mom and Diane's mom *did* talk and it was decided that A.J. and I could hang out at the hotel the night before.

That Tuesday afternoon was like something out of a bad movie. I changed my clothes three times. First, I wanted to wear sweats and my Mets jacket so I would look…well, I'm not sure how I would look. Like a baseball player, I guess.

Then I thought that was stupid and put on jeans and a button-down plaid shirt that I kept untucked. But I thought that made me look…I don't know. I guess Dad-like.

I got out of that and put on khaki pants, black shoes and a navy-blue pullover sweater. Looking in the mirror, I thought I looked smart but athletic, young but not childish, and confident but accessible.

I was just tying my shoes when I got a text from A.J. I opened it and it was a picture of him. *He* was in khakis, black shoes with Velcro laces and a heavy-cotton black shirt. I texted **Great minds think alike** and he replied **So do yours and mine.**

The Redfern was only about five miles from our place. The plan was that my mom would take us there around four-thirty and we could hang out in the lobby as long as we wanted or until we got bored. When it was time to go, we'd just call home and someone would pick us up. Diane's mom worked at the travel desk, right off the registration table, and could keep an eye on us. She would also let us know if she heard of any doings by Spike and would steer us his way.

A.J.'s mom drove us, reminding us to be polite to Diane's mom and not to "bother that nice Mr. Spike too much". I wanted to take our Mets Yearbooks and *People* magazines for Spike to autograph, but A.J. thought that wasn't cool, so we left them home.

The Redfern was one of those places that was pretty new but tried to look old. It was designed to look like a big, old Colonial house, but one with about fifty bedrooms. We stepped through the double-wooden doors, which were propped open, and stepped into the lobby.

We climbed out of the car and each gave A.J.'s mom a kiss goodbye in our excitement. We piled into the lobby and if excitement gave off a scent, you could smell us all the way to Outer Mongolia. (Which reminds me. Is there an Inner Mongolia? Don't know. Just asking.)

The lobby was a lot like the outside, with prints of maritime paintings and a few of horses and sunsets. Hidden speakers played some classical music and the room was filled with the reddish afternoon sunshine.

Diane's mom waved us over. She worked at a large desk of glass and chrome with a sign that said TRAVEL hanging over it. She was about the same age as our moms, I guess, with light red hair pulled back in a ponytail. She wore a gray pantsuit and smiled at us.

"You must be Nancy's brothers," she said.

Not the way I wanted to be remembered, but I figured this was the wrong time to argue. A.J. the same, since we both just nodded. Grinning like idiots.

She pointed at overstuffed armchairs in the corner of the lobby. "You boys just wait there, and keep quiet," she said. "I don't want to get in trouble," she added, nodding to the woman behind the reception desk.

A.J. said we would. Then, Diane's mom lowered her voice and leaned closer. "There's a man here, Mr. Steppinitis, who is Spike's manager. I heard him telling Spike to stay in and keep out of trouble. So, if he's around when I see Spike, I'll give you a signal."

We nodded again and moved like spies in enemy country to the armchairs. We sat and A.J. kept scanning the lobby, his eyes like homing devices.

Our excitement lasted a good two hours. Near the end of three hours, it was a lot lower. I mean...a *lot* lower. It was just after seven-thirty when I suggested to A.J. that maybe we should just skip it and see Spike at the Blu-ray event tomorrow when he stood up and said, "Let's get a breath of air."

We stepped outside and the sun was just going down. It was one of those warm spring evenings where the first thing you smell is the trees and the first thing you feel is the gentle breeze. A.J. stretched, his long body bending backwards as he cracked his back. I just yawned.

"Wanna go home?" I asked.

"Just a little while longer," he said.

"Let's walk," I said.

"Okay, but not long," he said. "I don't want to miss him."

We turned right and went around the side of the building, then turned again and walked along the back. In the rear of the Redfern was a large parking lot and moths were already gathering around the streetlights that were designed to look old. We were about to turn again to the far side of the building when someone called us.

"Hey kid," a voice said.

A.J. and I looked at each other, then looked around the parking lot. Nobody.

We shrugged and turned.

"Hey kid!" the voice said again. "Up here!"

A.J. and I stopped and looked up.

And there, leaning out of a second story window, was Spike, Jayson Tuttman, The Emperor of First Base.

And he was calling us.

I pointed at myself. "Us?" I gulped.

Spike was leaning out the window, his blond hair falling around his forehead in thick tufts. He had on a tight silk body shirt that showed off all his muscles and his green eyes flashed bright in the streetlights.

"Who do you think I mean?" he said. He pointed at A.J. "You, come over here." He pointed at me. "And you, catch this."

He threw a dark jacket out of the window. I caught it without thinking, looking up at him as I'm sure guys looked up at the first airplane ever. I held the jacket close against me.

A.J. stood under the window.

"Kid," Spike said, "you look like a strong, healthy boy. Stand close against the wall."

A.J. pressed his chest against the brick, turning his face so his cheek brushed against it.

"No, stupid. Turn around and put your back against it."

A.J. turned and pressed against the wall, standing as straight as he could.

Spike lowered himself out of the window, holding onto the sill. His arms bulged as he lowered himself, the toes of his boots stretched down toward A.J.

One boot clocked A.J. on the top of the head, then he managed to plant one foot on each of his shoulders.

"Steady, kid," he said.

He let go of the sill, palms flat against the wall now.

"Kid," he said to me. "Come over here and reach up."

I realized that my mouth was open. I closed it and came over.

"Reach up and gimme a hand."

I reached up and Spike bent sideways to take my hand. His grip was like iron. I heard A.J. groan a bit under the weight.

"I'm too important to get hurt," he said, balancing himself on my hand before jumping off of A.J.'s shoulders.

Spike landed hard beside me, his boots crunching in the gravel around us. He straightened up and started brushing himself off.

We just stood there looking.

"Spike," A.J. said. No points for originality, but factually correct.

"The Emperor of First Base," I added, not doing much better than A.J.

A.J. put out his hand and Spike shook it, then wiped his palm on his shirt.

I put out my hand. He shook it and said, "Gimme my jacket."

"My name is Thom Wilcox and this is A.J. Lopez," I said. "We're your two biggest fans."

"Great, kid," he said. "Gimme my jacket."

"We were the guys with the banner."

"Cool," he said. "Gimme my jacket."

"We are here because we wanted to get a chance to meet you," I gushed. "A.J. here is a first baseman and he looks just like you."

Spike turned and gave A.J. another look. Somehow, I don't think he was impressed by what he saw. He turned to me again and leaned closer. "Give. Me. My. Jacket."

"Oh," I said, stupidly. I handed it back.

He took it from my grasp as if I had tried to run off with it. As he shook it out, I had a good chance to get a closer look at him.

He was everything he was in his poster. Very tall – even a little taller than A.J., and A.J. towered over me – very handsome with thick blond hair and those biceps that seem to writhe whenever he moved his arms. His face was handsome, but he did not seem to be very warm.

He put his jacket on and said, "You kids got wheels?"

"Wheels?" A.J. asked.

"A car?" he explained. Like we were stupid.

"Our mom dropped us off," I said. No help there.

"I need to get out for a while," he said. "My manager is here and—"

"Mr. Steppinitis," I said, ever helpful.

Spike lurched and grabbed the front of my shirt, pulling me close to his face. I could feel his breath on my cheek when he growled, "What do you know of Steppinitis?"

"Nothing!" I bleated.

"We just heard that your manager was here," A.J. said, coming closer.

Spike let go of me, his face suspicious. Then he brushed the front of my shirt. "Sorry kid. Stuff you wouldn't understand." He looked around the parking lot. "You from around this piss hole?"

A.J. and I exchanged looks. "We live here."

"Great," he said. He pointed at A.J. "You're my wingman for tonight." He pointed at me. "You can come, but keep your mouth shut." He started walking away from us. "C'mon. I have a car around here somewhere."

A.J. and I hesitated for an instant, but only an instant. In a second we were chasing after him like puppies.

Spike was fishing around his jacket pockets when he found a car key fob. He took it out and pressed the button a few times until a new silver Hyundai Elantra lit up. Spike muttered a few swear words under his breath while talking about rental cars and led the way.

He stepped into the driver's seat and A.J. took the passenger side. I piled into the back.

A.J. was dutifully putting on his seatbelt while Spike started the car. "All right, we party tonight." Spike said. "What place is happening?"

"Like what?" I asked.

"I didn't ask you," he said. "If you're staying in the car, keep your mouth shut."

A.J. looked at him. "Well," he said. "The Rusty Nail is nice."

102

"How would you know?" I asked. Spike turned and gave me another dirty look.

"I heard," A.J. said.

"Lead the way."

Spike pulled out of the parking lot and took the road. We stopped for a moment at a 7-Eleven, where he picked up a pack of Lucky Strikes, and soon the car filled with smoke.

He handed the pack to A.J. "Keep these in your pocket. Steppinitis doesn't want me smoking, so say it's yours if you're asked anything. Okay?"

A.J. nodded and put the pack in his pocket.

"You can have one, if you want."

A.J. shot me a look, then slid a cigarette out of the pack. Spike tossed him a pack of matches and he lit up, trying hard to look like he smoked every day. After a puff, he just held it in his hand. Whenever Spike said something, A.J. would gesture with his cigarette, as if they were "just guys".

"Steppinitis has been on my case for weeks," Spike said. "You'd think he owns me. But I'm Mr. Excitement. The Emperor of First Base. Spike. The game happens because of me, you know?"

A.J. gestured with the cigarette in a way that said, *Of course. That's just like Steppinitis.*

"He's in for a big surprise when my contract is up," Spike said. "I'm not putting up with this anymore."

A.J. gestured again. *That's only natural,* he seemed to say.

"And next time I pose for one of those goddamn posters," he added, "he only gets five percent on sales. You get me. Only. Five. Percent."

A.J. shrugged, gesturing with his cigarette. He gestured, *It seems only fair.*

The Rusty Nail is a small pub not far from the park. Spike pulled into the lot and opened the door, throwing his cigarette on the ground. He slammed the car door and ushered us to the entrance.

I hadn't been inside the Rusty Nail before—I had never been inside of *any* bar, for that matter—I could tell it was a nice place. Like a lot of restaurants and shops in Stony Brook, it had a nautical air, and was decorated with ship's wheels, old maps, a couple of maritime prints and one huge model ship suspended over the bar. Hanging near the door were a series of oars, each with the name of a local yacht etched on their sides.

Spike looked around. He was not impressed. "This is it?"

A.J. looked around, wondering what was wrong with it. "Yeah."

Spike came closer to him, voice lower. "Kid. I want drinks and I want girls. You too dumb to understand that? My mother would go to this place."

"Sorry," was the best A.J. could manage.

A nice-looking lady with short black hair stood behind the car and came closer. "You can sit anywhere at the bar," she said, "or grab a table over there."

Spike said something to her that was very rude and left. A.J. and I looked at her apologetically and followed.

He was already stepping into the car when we caught up and climbed in behind him.

"Where to now?" A.J. asked.

"Kid," Spike said, backing up too quickly for such a small lot, "we're heading back to civilization."

I knew I was supposed to be quiet, but I couldn't help it. "Where's that?"

"New York, butthole," he said.

And we drove into the night.

Chapter Six

So, we drove to New York City.

If I live to be one hundred, I'll never forget that drive. Spike found an oldies radio station and put that on. It takes a little more than ninety minutes to get from Stony Brook to the heart of New York, and Spike took the whole thing at top speed, chain smoking cigarettes and singing Beach Boys songs at the top of his lungs.

We took the Long Island Expressway to the Midtown Tunnel and entered New York in the mid-Thirties. Spike knew exactly where he wanted to go as he headed uptown and then put the Elantra in a garage near Times Square.

When A.J. and I went to the city, we mostly saw Queens and the area around Citi Stadium, so being in the heart of Manhattan at night was a *huge* deal. It was now nearly eight o'clock at night, and the theaters and attractions at Times Square were lit so brightly that it looked like a little pocket of daylight in the center of the darkest night. The noise of the city came to us through the car windows, and when we got out of the Elantra at the garage, we could almost feel the energy of the city like an electric current.

A.J. and I stood by the car while Spike went to the window and got his rental ticket. I pulled my phone and noted the time.

"Maybe we should call home?" I suggested.

"Not yet," A.J. said. "Let's wait and see."

Wait and see what? I wondered, but said nothing.

Spike led us out the garage, both of us doing our best to keep up. He said we were to be his *wingmen*. I didn't know exactly what that meant, but figured it entailed sticking close to him.

We went down to the mid-Thirties and moved far west until we came upon a tiny little bar that was nestled off of Ninth Avenue. We could hear music from inside more than half a block away.

There was a tall black man standing at the door in a gray suit with a turtle-neck shirt. His arms were folded and he looked pretty forbidding.

Spike walked up and said hello and the tall man smiled and moved aside from the door. We were following him in when the man laid a hand on each of our shoulders.

"Where you dudes think you're going?" he growled.

Spike turned. "They're with me."

"They legal?"

"Sure," Spike said, lying about our age in a heartbeat. "They're just starting in the Minors." He actually pried the tall man's hand from A.J.'s shoulder and said, "That's A.C.

Going to be a big ballplayer." He pointed to me. "That's my friend D.C."

Close enough, I thought.

"You boys got ID?" the giant asked.

ID for A.C. and D.C. I thought. Spike said. "Steppinitis."

The giant nodded and released me. "Go ahead."

We stepped inside and the noise almost knocked me off my feet. I had never heard music so loud. I could feel the ground vibrating under me like it was a living thing.

The bar was darkly lit except for some lights spinning overhead which turned the place blue, then red, the yellow, then blue again. There was a dance floor packed with gyrating people, heaving and breathing like they were a single, living breathing thing.

Spike passed the bar and tons of guys patted him on the shoulder or gave him the high five. When he was done being adored he led us to a small table up a few stairs and we sat. He said something to A.J., who leaned-in closer to hear it. I couldn't hear a thing but the music.

After a few minutes a waitress came up to us. She was in jeans slung low with a wide belt and wore a halter top that was tied in a bow at her tummy. Spike grinned broadly and said something to her, then pointed at me and A.J.

She said something, I couldn't catch all of it, but I did hear, "ID?"

Spike shouted something back at her over the noise. I think it was, "I'm Jayson Tuttman!"

Almost automatically I heard myself yell, "He's Spike!"

A.J. added, "The Emperor of First Base."

She looked at all of us. I couldn't tell what she was thinking, but she just shrugged and walked off. In only a few minutes she came back with a tray and placed two glasses in front of each of us. One was a shot glass filled with amber liquid and the other was a tall, frosted glass of beer.

Spike shouted something that sounded like "Boilermaker."

A.J. and I exchanged looks, then turned to watch Spike.

Spike picked up the shot glass and swallowed its contents in one gulp. He then picked up the beer and took a long, deep swallow. He put the glass down and, despite the noise of the music, I heard it thud against the table top.

A.J. took the shot glass and did likewise. I saw his eyes grow wide for a moment, but he kept his face neutral. Then he grabbed the beer and drank nearly half of it.

Both pairs of eyes turned toward me. I lifted the shot glass and swallowed the stuff down. There was a burning in my throat and my tongue turned to lava. I grabbed my neck and started coughing while A.J. hammered on my back. Before I was able to breathe again, Spike pushed the beer at me and I started to drink.

I drank half of the beer before the burning stopped and I could breathe again. I put the glass down and suddenly…the world changed.

The inside of my head felt as if it was filled with hundreds of balloons, and they started popping one after another. I could feel my heart beating in my chest and the noise of the music was getting louder and the room was getting darker. I realized I was breathing through my mouth.

I saw Spike gesture to the waitress, who was a good thirty feet from us. He swung his hand around, then held up three fingers.

I held up a hand but he said something that was clouded by the music.

I took my beer and looked around the room. I could never make out the lyrics of the music, but my heartbeat started to move in time with the rhythm. My temples started to pound.

I looked and saw A.J. leaning forward and nodding as Spike was shouting something in his ear. I had only been here for fifteen minutes, and already I wanted out.

Then, something in my back pocket vibrated.

I pulled out my phone and saw that it was my father calling. If I was going to own up to the truth, now was as good a time as any.

I hit ANSWER and put the phone to my ear.

I kinda, sorta, maybe heard my dad say something, but couldn't be sure. I yelled, "Dad, I can't hear you." This went on for a minute or two, me not hearing and then me shouting, before the connection cut off. I was going to text him when the waitress came back with the drinks.

A.J. put a hand on my phone and motioned me to put it back in my pocket. I did and looked down at our drinks.

Spike and A.J. clinked shot glasses together in a toast that I didn't catch and then swallowed them down. Both touched beer glasses in a salute before drinking their beer. They had only known each other for about two hours and A.J. already seemed to like him better than me. And that really pissed me off.

I picked up my shot glass and smelled the whiskey. My gut flipped over and I put it down. Spike and A.J. were looking, with A.J. motioning, *drink up*.

What the hell, I thought. I held my breath and swallowed the drink, then washed it down with my fresh beer.

Where the first shot made my head feel like a lot of balloons popping, this one had almost the opposite effect. As soon as the beer made its way through, my head felt like it was filled with cold oatmeal. I felt my forehead grow clammy and little beads of sweat break out all over me.

Even worse, the back of my tongue felt heavy and yucky. It didn't help that I was also a little dizzy.

My phone was buzzing again in my pants and I decided this might be a good time to look at it.

It was a couple of texts from dad. The first was: WHERE ARE YOU? This was followed by: CALLED THE HOTEL AND YOU'RE NOT THERE. The last was: WORRIED. ANSWER NOW.

I hit reply and used swipe to type as my fingers were…mushy. I wrote: OUT WITH SPIKE! TOUCH BASE SOON.

Then I put the phone in my pocket, determined not to think about it for a few minutes. I looked up at A.J. and Spike and they were thick as thieves, shouting stuff into each other's ear to be heard over the music. I had no idea what they were talking about. I was sure it wasn't about me.

The club lights were now flashing with a terrible intensity, and my head was pounding in time with them. I looked around at the people there, then turned back to the table to find A.J. sitting there alone.

I shrugged my shoulders and put up my hands.

A.J. pointed in the distance. I saw Spike at the bar surrounded by friends, bending low on the bar top with a folded bill in his hand. He stood up straight and the people around him were laughing.

I pulled out my phone and texted A.J., even though he wasn't three feet away from me. I was worried that he wouldn't be able to hear me.

MY DAD HAS BEEN CALLING, I wrote

A.J. looked up from his phone and just nodded at me.

WHAT SHOULD WE DO? I wrote.

He texted back. JUST BE COOL.

That was easy for him to say. The weird feeling in my head was migrating down to my stomach. I put my head down on the table for a moment and things started swimming in the blackness.

Next thing I know, I get a noogie at the back of my head. It's Spike, and he's sitting down again next to A.J., sniffling and patting white powder from his nose. I rubbed my head where his knuckles rapped against my skull.

Spike laughed and A.J. laughed too. So I laughed, but I didn't find it very funny.

The waitress came up and Spike said something to her. As she was leaving he reached out and touched her on the behind and she turned and looked daggers at him. Spike just laughed.

That was it—my gut had enough. I slowly got to my feet, feeling dizzy with the sense of heaviness at the back of my tongue worse than before. I gripped the back of the chair as I focused and saw what I thought was the door to the men's room. Walking with careful steps, I made my way to it. With the lights, the noise and all the people around me, in some weird way I felt like I was walking through water.

I was just at the door when I realized I needed to run. I pushed the door open and ran to the first sink in a row of them and barfed like I had never barfed before. It's not just that I emptied out my stomach—I had emptied out everything from my toes on up. Wave after wave of puke shot out of me until I was just dry-heaving a little bit of bile.

When I was done I looked up blearily at a man standing at the sink next to me, staring at me in shock. He was a tall black man, with short hair and a gold chain that matched his dark yellow pants. "I knew New York made people sick," he said.

The worst part of it was that whatever I had barfed up clogged the sink, and all that mess wasn't going down the drain. I moved down the line to a sink further away and ran cold water over my hands and face. Then I cupped my hands and rinsed out my mouth; it was burning from whatever I had brought up.

I realized that the guy who had been standing next to me before was still looking at me. I just nodded and said, "I'm alright."

He moved a little closer. Suddenly, I got a little nervous and moved back a step.

He noticed and stopped, smiling weakly. "Relax. Just checking on you." He pulled several paper towels from the overhead rack and handed them to me. "Wipe yourself off."

I dried my hands and face, him watching me all the time. I balled the towels in my fist and looked for the trash can.

He just reached out and I put them in his fist. He went near the door and threw them into the trash can. He turned and asked, "Are you old enough to be here?"

First I shook my head, but then I lowered my voice and said, "Yeah."

"You with some friends?"

"Yes."

"You not driving?"

"No," I said. "I'm here with Jayson Tuttman. Spike," I said. "You know. The Emperor of First Base. From the Mets."

"He's here a lot." The man shook his head, like I said I was there with Sauron, the Dark Lord of Mordor. "Go home and don't get your ass in trouble."

"Yes," I said, and it sounded like the first intelligent thing anyone said that night. I don't know if it was the throwing up, or the cool water, or the good sense this guy was giving me, but suddenly my head started to clear (The bathroom smelled terrible, thanks to me, and that was no help. But...still). I moved to the door, patting the man on the arm as I passed, and went back out into the club.

I saw A.J. and Spike at the table. Both were nodding to the music and surveying the room like they owned it. I hadn't been this mad at A.J. since he hit me with that plastic hammer back in the playpen. For a hot minute, I considered walking out, calling dad and telling him what happened, and then getting a train home. It was the only sane thing to do.

What stopped me? Actually, it was that encounter with the guy in the bathroom. I had thought of the Dark Lord of Mordor, and my brain instantly went into *Lord of the Rings* mode. I had every intention of walking away until I thought of Samwise Gamgee.

For those of you who haven't read *Lord of the Rings* (all two of you), I should explain. There are all kinds of heroes in the *Rings*, and just a list of them—starting with Frodo and Bilbo and Gimli and Aragorn—would fill the pages of a small book. But the *real* hero is the little hobbit, Samwise Gamgee.

Samwise is a gardener and he is also Frodo's loyal friend. He stays with him through the darkest and most terrible moments of his life. He's one of the very few who do not feel the terrible influence and dark power of the ring. And he's the guy who pulls Frodo's fat out of the fire time and again. Yeah, Frodo is "the hero" but without Samwise, the hero would end up somewhere in the volcanic pits of Mount Doom.

For most readers, Aragon and Boromir are the big, strong hero types that everyone wants to be. But if you're lucky and pay close attention to life…you end up like Samwise

Gamgee. And tonight, I figured I had better be lucky and pay close attention, because A.J. was going to need a Samwise Gamgee.

I made my way through the crowds back to the table just as the waitress was putting our third round of boilermakers on the table. A.J. and Spike lifted their whiskey glasses and toasted again before downing them in a gulp. Then both washed them down with some beer. A.J. was beginning to look a little glassy eyed. He burped (loud enough to be heard over the music) and leaned over to me.

"You okay?" he shouted into my ear.

I gave him a thumb's up.

"Drink up," Spike said.

I nodded. "I'm done!" I shouted back.

Spike just leaned over and took up my glass and swallowed it down; he also finished my beer when he was done with his.

We were there for a long time before Spike realized he'd had enough and it was time to hit the next place. He went to the bar and pulled out his wallet to pay the bill.

He led us out of the bar and onto the street. I was so relieved to be outside that my head *popped* with a sense of relief, like a giant zit. A.J. smiled dumbly and staggered back a step.

I reached out for him, but Spike clamped an iron hand around A.J.'s arm and pulled him upright. "Don't wimp out, dude," he said. "Like your friend here."

"I think I need something to eat," A.J. said.

"Just where we're going." Pulling A.J. along by the arm, we headed back to Ninth Avenue and turned uptown. The city, if anything, seemed more packed than it did before. I wondered if anyone there ever went to bed.

In a few blocks we hit a restaurant called Martinelli's. There were a lot of tables outside, despite the cool spring night. Spike, however, went up to the little lectern up front where a man in a jacket and tie stood.

"Table for three," he said. "*Now.*"

The man looked down at a binder on the lectern. "Do you have a reservation?"

"You kidding? You know who I am?"

"This is Spike," A.J. gurgled. "From the Mets."

"The Emperor of First Base," I added, without my usual enthusiasm.

I don't think the man knew what we were talking about. Spike reached into his pants pocket and pulled out two twenty-dollar bills. *That* the man understood. "This way, please," he said, leading us inside the restaurant.

Martinelli's is this nice little Italian restaurant; the kind that you picture in your mind when you think *nice little Italian restaurant*. It had red-and-white checked tablecloths,

Chianti bottles with multi-colored candles sticking out of them, and prints featuring Italian landscapes. The guy showed us to this nice, private table in the corner and told us that our waiter will be with us presently.

And he was. The waiter was a small, trim man with curly hair and big liquid brown eyes. He wore a white shirt and black pants, and had little red elastic bands around his biceps. I thought he was cute.

Faggot, Robert Dillworth said.

The waiter gave us menus and before he even looked at them, Spike said, "Bring a bottle of the house red."

The waiter nodded and left. Spike buried his nose in the menu and I watched as A.J. blinked multiple times to focus his vision. He burped again…that sounded kinda ominous to me.

The waiter returned with a basket of bread and some butter. Spike grabbed the biggest piece for himself and slathered it with butter. A.J. took a piece and started absently chewing on it. I took a piece myself, it helped take the taste of bile out of my mouth.

"So Spike," A.J. said, "this one of your favorite places?"

Spike scanned the restaurant. "Look around. Lotta girls here."

Spike's eyes rested on a blond woman about five tables away, quietly eating dinner beside a man with a mustache. She was very pretty and her hair fell over her shoulders in thick folds. She felt Spike's eyes on her and she looked up before giving him an awkward smile.

"Look at the hooters on that one," Spike whispered. "She's a honey."

A.J. looked, but I'm not sure his eyes were focused. "A honey," he said.

"Whattaya think?" he asked me.

I felt my eyes grow wide as I struggled for an answer. "Yeah," I said.

Spike turned to A.J. with a comic grin. "Not sure about your friend here. Sure he don't like guys?"

Faggot, Robert Dillworth said

A.J. nodded. "No. He's fine."

I felt my pants vibrate again. I pulled my phone from my back pocket. My dad had texted, YOU NEED TO CALL HOME NOW!

So, this was a defining moment, I thought. I could call my dad, or be Samwise and get a boatload of trouble in the process. I opted for Samwise and put my phone in my back pocket.

The waiter came with a bottle of red wine and one wine glass, looking pointedly at both me and A.J. He put the wine glass in front of Spike and poured out just a drop. Spike sipped it and nodded.

The waiter filled his glass, put down the bottle and walked away. Spike picked up the bottle and poured some wine into A.J.'s empty water glass.

"Drink up," he said. "Prohibition's over."

He didn't offer me any, and that was fine by me. He and A.J. drank up. When Spike put down his glass he said, "You jerks are okay."

"Gee," I said. "Thanks."

"First I thought Steppinitis set you on my ass. To watch me, you know."

I could just imagine, I thought.

"But I see you just want some fun." He turned back to the menu. "Order what you want. Party's on me."

It suddenly dawned on me that I was hungry. Especially after barfing all of my guts out. I looked over the menu. There were a lot of expensive things there, but I didn't want to take advantage of Spike paying for everything. There was a moderately priced dish of chicken parmesan and spaghetti. I settled on that.

When the waiter came, I made my order and thanked him. A.J. ordered the same. Spike wanted to start with mussels, then with a calzone, and finally ending up with veal scaloppini. I figured if he could eat all that, he had to be part ox.

"So," I said, always ready to get the ball rolling, "how'd you end up with the Mets?"

Spike took a long swallow of wine. "Didn't you read about it in the Yearbook?" he asked. "After all, you're my two biggest fans. Right?"

There was something about the way he said *my two biggest fans* that annoyed me, but I didn't say anything about that. Instead I asked, "Well, we're curious because A.J. is a really good first baseman."

"Really?" Spike was pouring himself more wine. "How good?"

"The best at our school," I said.

He just smiled at that. Then, turning to A.J. he asked, "You think you got what it takes to hit the Major Leagues?"

Suddenly A.J. was sitting up straight. "Yes." He burped. "That is, yes, Spike."

Spike leaned forward, as if he was going to share with us the secrets of all the cosmos. "Let me tell you two little wimps something," he said. "You can play a good game of ball with your friends or at school, but that don't count for squat in the Major Leagues. There's a reason they're the majors, jerkoffs. It's hard," he said, taking another sip of wine. "Friggin' *hard*."

"Well, everyone has got to start somewhere, right?" I asked. "Even you had to start somewhere, right?"

He pointed a finger under my chin. "Don't you tell me what I did or didn't have to do," he growled. "You think this is easy? Having to pull a team full of losers and schmucks out of the basement all by yourself? Putting up with questions from little pissants like you? Steppinitis thinks he can play me like a puppet, but that putz has another thing coming."

Normally, I'm not happy to be called a wimp, jerkoff or pissant. Normally, I would walk away. Normally, A.J. wouldn't put up with it either (Normally, I don't start every sentence with *normally*). But A.J. was listening as if this was some kind of revelation that he had searched for his whole life. I kept my mouth shut.

"Sorry," A.J. said. Whether he was sorry for being a wimp, a jerkoff or pissant, I was unsure.

Spike smacked him on the shoulder. Probably harder than he should have, because A.J.'s glassy eyes cleared for an instant in pain. "Don't worry," Spike said. "You assholes are okay."

"Thanks."

"But if A.J. had what it takes," I started. Before he could cut me off, I added, "And I understand that's rare! But if he did, what would someone with all your experience and knowledge of the game recommend?"

Spike turned to A.J. "He your agent?"

"I'm Samwise Gamgee," I muttered.

"What?" Spike asked. I don't think A.J. heard me though.

"Nothing," I said.

The waiter brought our food. Spike and A.J. dived into the mussels. I was starved, but after getting sick in the bar I didn't think mussels were a good idea. I chewed on more bread as the waiter brought the calzone. This was a round, bready thing sliced down the center, stuffed with hot, white cheese and thick clumps of ham. I passed on that, as well, though A.J. and Spike were wolfing it down.

A.J. burped again. This was so loud, people at other tables turned to look. Spike used it as an opportunity to look at the blonde woman at the other table.

"So, what do you think?" A.J. asked.

"I think she's hot," Spike said.

"I mean," A.J. was making an effort to speak clearly through all the booze, "what advice can you give me?"

"Be like me," Spike said, shoveling a forkful of veal into his mouth. "Play hard and train every day. Think about the game and nothing else. And I mean *nothing* else. Don't worry about the other guy, 'cause he ain't worrying about you. And make sure that when you play, play to win."

I twirled some spaghetti onto my fork, listening.

"And hold onto what you got," he added, mouth full. "When you got something—anything—the whole world tries to take it away from you. Hold onto it and make sure it pays out the best for you."

"Should A.J. take lessons or find a personal coach?" I asked.

Spike nodded, dipping bread into his gravy and taking a bite. "Anything that gives you the edge. And take care of yourself. An athlete's one asset is his body and his health." He took another drink of wine. "Keep yourself in shape and don't abuse it."

A.J. nodded, taking another sip of wine himself.

Spike refilled his glass, face clouded with thought. He drank a whole glass in a gulp, then refilled again. Looking into space he said, "And remember, jerkoffs. You're alone. You're completely, totally, friggin' *alone*. Ain't no one going to be there for you, except when you make it to the top. And then once you're there, just to take it away from you."

I don't know what A.J. made of this, but I could almost feel my heart breaking for Spike. Yeah, he was a major jerk. But maybe even major jerks start out as victims of something.

To his credit, he did spend the rest of dinner telling A.J. about the proper stance for throwing, about how to distribute his weight at the plate, and what he had learned about getting a man out. A.J.'s head was like a sponge, getting bigger with everything Spike spilled out.

Our plates were cleared and when that was done the cute waiter...

Faggot, Robert Dillworth said.

...asked if we wanted dessert. Spike told him to bring dessert menus and, when the man left, Spike nodded towards the blonde woman at the other table and said, "That's what I want for dessert."

A.J. leered with him (Or, at least, leered as best he could. It was his first try).

We all ordered dessert. I had rice pudding, mainly because there is no type of pudding I can resist. A.J. and Spike had something called tiramisu, which looked like a cross between cake and pudding.

My phone vibrated and I pulled it from my back pocket. Dad texted, JUST LET ME KNOW YOU'RE ALRIGHT.

I typed ALL GOOD, and put it back in my pocket.

"Now, peckerheads," he said, taking the last forkful of tiramisu. "Here's where you pay for dinner."

My heart stopped. I don't know about A.J., but I didn't have any money.

A.J. was on the same wavelength. "Ah…" he started.

"No," Spike said. "Payback with a favor."

"What kind of favor?" I'm nothing if not direct.

Spike kept his eyes on the blond woman a few tables away. "I'm thinking."

Whatever he was thinking was interrupted by the waiter, who brought the bill. Still looking at the woman, he pulled his wallet from his back pocket and put his credit card on the tray without looking at the tab.

"I'm having a brainstorm," he said.

I was so tired myself that the closest I could have come to a brainstorm at that moment was a slight drizzle. And for some reason, Spike having a brainstorm was more than enough to make me nervous.

A.J. also had me worried. He seemed in better shape after he had something to eat, but his whole body would still rack with these violent burps. And while his eyes were less glassy, I wouldn't want Mr. Lopez to catch him in this condition. Nor even his mom.

The waiter came back with the credit card and receipt. Spike signed it and handed it back. "Wait!" he said, putting his wallet away and reaching into his front pocket. He sorted some bills and then held up four fifty-dollar bills.

The waiter certainly noticed that.

"Here's a two-hundred-dollar tip," Spike said. "But you have to do something for me."

"Sir?" The waiter seemed as suspicious as I was.

Spike turned his head and gave the restaurant the once over. He nodded towards the men's room, and said to me and the waiter, "You, and you, c'm'over here."

Spike got up and led us into a small alcove that separated the bathrooms from the rest of the restaurant. The entranceway was closed off by a hanging curtain of multicolored beads. Spike parted the beads and we had a hidden council of war.

"Get the kid an apron and some of those arm bands," he told the waiter. "And a tray with something on it. I don't care what—dirty dishes, glasses of water, knock yourself out. And keep your mouth shut."

The waiter thought for a moment. I could almost hear the wheels turning in his head. "No, sir. Thank you, I can't."

I knew I liked him.

Spike fanned him with the four fifty-dollar bills. "Dude. Who else is going to tip you two hundred bucks?" And then he grinned, as if it was all fun and games anyway. "And you know who I am?"

Spike then nodded to me.

"Jayson Tuttman," I said, sounding like an answering machine. "Spike. The Emperor of First Base." He should just have a sign made.

The waiter looked from me to the money, then snatched the money. He wadded the bills into his pocket and said, "Just give me a moment."

I watched the waiter head back into the kitchen, then turned to Spike.

"What do you want me to do?"

Spike grinned. "Wait for it. It'll be good."

I looked back at our table. A.J. sat there alone. My impulse was to just take him by the hand, the way he did that first day in kindergarten, and lead him away. I didn't think he would let me.

Soon the waiter came back holding a tray with water glasses and something draped over his free arm. He passed through the beaded curtain.

"Hurry," he said. "I could get fired for this."

Spike took the apron from the waiter and spun me around like a store window dummy. Next thing I knew, he had the apron on me. He was then sliding these red arm bands up my biceps—they matched the waiter's perfectly. Spike then took the tray from the waiter and said, "Get lost."

The waiter left and Spike handed me the tray.

"No, dummy," he said. "Don't hold it like that. Like *this*." He made a right angle with his arm and flattened his hand so the tray rested on it like a table.

I did that. All was ready.

Spike turned me towards the interior of the restaurant. He stood behind me, hands on my shoulders and lips to my ear so I could feel his breath when he spoke.

"I want you to go in there, but walk along the side of the wall. Don't draw attention to yourself. Make for the table with the blond with the hooters," he said, his breath hot and rank. "When you pass behind the man, *bang*, accidently drop the tray on his lap."

I couldn't help it. I turned around and looked at him. "You," I said, "are a mental case."

"Make like a Nike, peckerhead," he said, pushing me through the beads, "and just do it."

I barreled through the beaded curtains, just barely keeping the tray of water glasses upright. A.J. turned as I entered the room and blinked multiple times, as if his eyes were playing tricks on him.

If only they were.

I moved into the interior of the restaurant and then glided – inconspicuously, I hoped – toward the inner wall. I smiled at some people at a table trying to get my attention as I passed, and moved closer to my objective.

The couple had finished their dessert and was now having coffee (This, by the way, is something that adults do that amazes me. They drink coffee to stay awake, and then they drink it right before bed. Go figure.). He was only about ten years older than me, with dark brown hair and a mustache. If I had seen him on the street, I would've guessed he was a pretty good guy. That made me feel all the worse.

The woman was listening to what he said but, to be honest, she did glance at the table where Spike had been sitting a few times. Did she wonder where the guy who had been staring at her went? Was she looking at A.J.? Or did she realize Spike was a celebrity? I thought my life would suddenly become a whole lot simpler if I could just ask.

I didn't plan *how* I was going to do this. Faced with the job…I just did it.

As I glided behind them I let the tray slide out of my hand, aiming the glasses to spill onto his lap.

They did.

The man was up and out of his seat in an instant.

"CHRIST!" he yelled.

The woman let out a little yelp.

The man stood there, the entire middle of his body drenched. The dark stain started under his ribcage and ended somewhere over his knees.

I picked a napkin from the table and furiously started brushing him off.

"I'm so sorry!"

He pushed me away and growled, "Jerk."

One of the real waiters was approaching and I decided I had better make tracks.

"Excuse me," I said and made for the kitchen. I saw the real waiter come and start helping the man dry off. As I neared the kitchen I turned and made a beeline for the ladies room.

Spike was already heading for the main part of the restaurant and his bulk must have partially hidden me. I parted the beads at the alcove, knocked on the ladies room door and, getting no answer, dived inside.

I heard the waiter leading the guy into the men's room with "we'll clean this right up" and "we're so sorry" and "this has never happened before".

I pulled off the apron and the armbands. I thought about chucking them in the trash but, heck, they weren't *mine*. So I balled them up and tossed them under the sink. Then I straightened my hair at the mirror before stepping outside.

As I parted the beads, I saw that Spike was already at the table with the blonde woman. A.J. was staring at me with his mouth open. If he was playing ball I'd think he could catch flies.

I darted to our table and took a chair next to him.

"What just happened?" he asked. Still a little too dazed for my taste.

"Watch," I said, nodding at Spike.

We turned and watched him in action. He was leaning near her and staring at her chest and she was staring back. We couldn't hear everything that was said, but I did catch, "Emperor of First Base".

She nodded as he spoke. When he finished, elbows on the table, he leaned forward as if they had been dating forever. She blinked and regarded him with loving eyes. She allowed him to move even closer.

That's when she did it.

As Spike came close enough to almost kiss her, she calmly lifted her coffee cup over his head and slowly poured it all over him.

Spike sat there as the coffee rained down on him, running in rivulets down his face, seeping down his shirt front and pooling in his lap.

Then, nonchalant as you please, she gently put her cup back on its saucer.

Spike sighed and took up her napkin, wiping his face. He stood, the front of his body one large coffee stain, and, looking at us, nodded towards the exit.

I didn't need to be told twice. I jumped to my feet and pulled A.J. up by the arm. Spike was striding towards the exit—us riding shotgun—as the man who got wet came back to the table. We heard her tell him something in a high-pitched voice.

That's when Spike put on the speed. He dashed through the front door, through the tables out front, and made for the cars parked at the curb. We brought up the rear, not sure what his play would be, but gamely following wherever he went.

Spike darted between two cars parked out front and dropped to his knees. A.J., always a little faster than me, nearly tripped over him. But, in a blink, we were on our knees, on either side of Spike, hiding behind a parked car.

He looked through the car windows and saw the mustached man step out of the restaurant. He looked left, then right, then took two steps forward. Seeing no sign of us, he cursed under his breath and went back inside.

Spike watched until he was sure that he was gone. He got to his feet and so did we. He looked at the huge plate-glass window that fronted the restaurant and said, "Peckerhead."

And that's when he saw it. It was right there on the floor, at his boot.

It was a bottle, probably left by some bum, lying on its side right near the tire of the car. A tiny thing—not more than twelve ounces or so. It said *Patron Citronge – Extra Fine Orange Liqueur.* That's one thing I can say about Manhattan: they have a high class of bum.

The bottle was empty and it must've had a cork at one time, because there were no grooves for a cap. A tiny drop of yellowish-orangeish liquid remained at the bottom.

Spike hefted the empty bottle for a moment and then let fly. I reached for his arm and almost stopped him, but that sure as heck wasn't good enough.

The tiny bottle sailed through the air like a bullet and landed square in the center of Martinelli's window. The bottle shattered with a sound like a gunshot. And the window cracked…completely. In a second, it looked like a giant spider-web, with hundreds (thousands? millions?) of long, white fractures spiraling through it.

It was like lightning had struck the ground inches in front of us. It was too loud, too fast and too amazing for it to register in our brains in that instant. And then…it did.

A.J. and me stood there, mouths open, when Spike pushed me aside and said, "Run!"

No kidding.

Spike ran into Ninth Avenue traffic, dodging cars as if he were going to tag them sliding into first base. A.J. and I were right behind him. I heard the voices of people behind us yelling and was too terrified to turn around and look.

Though not built for speed, Spike cut through traffic and roared down Ninth Avenue like a force of nature. A.J. was right behind and I brought up the rear. I was convinced that I was seconds away from being grabbed from behind and hauled away to jail. But after three blocks, Spike turned down a side street, reached the middle of the block, and ducked into another bar.

Spike barreled through the door like a battering ram, A.J. and then me spilling in after him. He led us to a table way in the back and we grabbed chairs.

I was silent for a full two minutes, watching A.J. and Spike catch their breath. They're faster, but I was the distance runner of the group. When they were able to relax, Spike took in his surroundings, leaned back in his chair and laughed.

And not just a laugh. A roar. He sat back and opened his mouth and laughed as if all his guts were spilling out.

A.J. looked at him for a moment, then he started laughing too.

I sat there.

As they were getting control of themselves, I looked around. I had lost track of the street numbers, but knew that we had gone downtown, so we were somewhere in the low-thirties or upper-twenties. My lifetime experience with bars was just what I had witnessed that very night, but somehow I didn't think they could get any darker than this. The walls were black slate, and people had written all kinds of things on them with white chalk. I saw the phrase SEX, DRUGS AND BUGS BUNNY CARTOONS, and stopped reading after that.

Some of the tables around us were occupied, others not. About fifty-fifty. There was a large bar that we passed when we exploded into the place; the bartender was watching us from a distance.

"Hey stupid," Spike turned to me. "Tell Eddie at the bar it's Spike and bring back three beers."

He sat there, blond hair plastered with spilled coffee, shirt and pants stained, with a stupid grin on his face. And here's the strangest thing. Even though he had already proven himself to be just about the biggest jerk in all the world, I *still* would've done most anything he asked me to.

I got up and after a few words with Eddie, came back with a tray holding three beers. For one crazy moment, I imagined *accidentally* dropping them on Spike's lap. But I didn't think beer would make a good chaser for coffee.

I put the beers on the table and dropped the tray on one of the empty tables. Spike and A.J. took up their glasses and toasted one another and started to drink. I sat in front of mine, leaving it untasted. I was looking at A.J. and my heart was breaking a little. I didn't know if it was because I was jealous, or because I thought he was making an ass out of himself.

"Drink up," Spike said.

"You have it," I said.

Spike pulled the glass closer to him and put it in front of A.J. "Here," he said. "Peckerhead doesn't want it."

A.J. shot me a look that lasted just an instant. Hurt, on my behalf? Disappointment in me? Resignation? I had no idea.

He finished his beer and then took mine. He didn't drink mine as quickly as he did the first one, but before long, it was gone.

After a little bit Eddie drifted back with a bowl of corn chips. Despite all that I ate at Martinelli's, I wanted to keep funneling food into me. I started picking at them absently as Spike ordered another round.

For the first time, A.J. started to talk to Spike instead of just listening. As the older man drank his beer, A.J. told him about his own ball playing, and about how we had painted a banner with his name that ended up on television. He even said something like, "This night is just about the greatest thing that ever happened to us."

I sat quiet and let A.J. have his fill. No matter what happened after this, he had a night on the town with Spike. It was like a war story…something he'd be able to talk about until he was an old man (and at the rate he was going, that would be in about six months). Spike was his hero, and here they were, bonding. I sat on my hands and kept my mouth shut. In a weird way, it was another gift from me to A.J.

But when he had talked himself out, I pulled my phone from my back pocket and checked the time. It read 10:18 PM. I didn't read the texts from my dad. I knew that I was beyond dead when I got home, so no need to worry about it now. But I did need to get A.J. home as soon as possible.

"A.J.," I said. "It's after ten."

"He adopt you or something?" Spike asked.

Though A.J.'s eyes had started getting glassy again, that seemed to focus them. "After ten?"

I nodded.

"Spike," I said. I felt I had to choose my words carefully, and I let each one out like I was lighting a match near a gas leak. "Spike, we had a great night. But our parents are already freaking out."

"Let 'em," he said. "It's good for them."

"Spike," A.J. said, his face all innocent. "We *do* have to go."

Spike sighed with bad grace and reached into his pocket. He dropped some bills on the table and we rose. We passed the bar and Spike waved absently to Eddie as we came to the door.

Spike turned to me. "Check and see that none of them dopes are looking for us."

I opened the door and scanned up and down the street. No dopes.

I turned and opened the door. "All clear."

We walked east to Eighth Avenue just to be on the safe side, not going west again until we were on the block with the garage. On the way, Spike asked, "We pulled one over on Steppinitis, didn't we?"

"We sure did," A.J. said.

"Damn straight," I said. I hate to be left out.

When we got to the garage, we followed Spike to the checkout window. It was a little room made out of cinderblocks with a desk-type tray surmounted by a thick, Plexiglas window that had little holes so you could hear what was said. Spike handed the man his ticket.

The garage guy, a solidly built black man, looked at Spike suspiciously. He tabulated the final cost and handed Spike the bill. Spike looked, pulled out some cash, and dropped it on the desk.

"Can I see your keys for a moment?" the man asked.

Spike blinked blearily, shrugged, then handed him the keys.

The man looked from Spike to A.J. Then his eyes settled on me.

"Kid," he said. "You got your license?"

"Yes." Permit, anyway.

"You drive."

"The hell he will!" Spike said.

"Pal," he said. "It's like this. You let the kid drive, or I hold the keys and call the cops. You decide."

"Do you know who I am?"

Spike turned to me.

"That's Jayson Tuttman," I said, now sounding like one of those computer recordings. "Spike. The Emperor of First Base. *Et cetera, et cetera.*"

"You going to be dead if you drive," the man said.

Spike gave him a dirty look. Then he gave me a dirty look for good measure. Then he shrugged, teetering a little on the balls of his feet.

The man handed me the keys.

A.J. burped; the great granddaddy of all burps. It echoed off the concrete walls of the garage like retreating thunder. I turned and looked at him. He wiped his mouth with the back of his hand and smiled sheepishly.

I led Spike and A.J. to the Elantra and hit the button to unlock the doors. I was afraid that Spike would want the keys back, but he walked around to the other side of the car and slumped in the back seat. A.J. opened the rear door nearest him and did the same.

I took the front. All alone.

I cautiously adjusted the mirrors and checked the GPS. The Redfern was on the list of recent addresses and I pointed us towards home.

Spike pulled the pack of Luckies from his jacket pocket and handed one to A.J. With shaky hands he lit both cigarettes and tossed the match on the carpet.

I had never driven in any city before, so driving in New York was, frankly, more than I wanted or expected. But I kept on the alert and carefully navigated the streets and the pedestrians. I just focused on the GPS and my surroundings and did my best to drive well.

Not that they made concentrating easy. Spike reached over the back seat and hit the radio. The oldies channel started blaring old rock even before I got out of the garage. Spike didn't just sing every song that came on, he *screamed* them, smoke curling around his head like a wreath. I was beginning to think he needed more than rehab. He needed an exorcist.

It was when I got on the Expressway that A.J. started in, too. When Spike sang, A.J. would join in as best he could. He didn't know the words to any of the songs (neither of us were into music), so he would just mumble gibberish at the top of his voice or harmonize with these strange sounds. They seemed to be enjoying themselves. At least someone was.

I took the Expressway calm and steady. There was once or twice when we passed police cars on the road and I tensed each time. I had my permit, but there should be an adult with me up front—and that adult should be sober. I was also unsure of driving on highways with a permit…normally I knew if I could or couldn't, but this wasn't a normal time and I couldn't remember. So I just drove as calmly and competently as I could when passing the police and hoped for the best.

Of course, my phone rang while I was driving. It was in my back pocket and I heard it ring again and again between my butt and the seat. Neither Spike nor A.J. said anything. For all I knew, they thought I was playing backup to their singing. I couldn't pull it out and talk while driving…and somehow, that made me feel worse.

And the part of my brain that wasn't concentrating on driving was focused on something maybe even more important—what came next. You see, what came next was more important than what we had just done. I had to come up with a story that would keep our respective parents from murdering us, and maybe even nudge us up a notch in their respect. It was not going to be easy, and I would have to do some pretty fancy thinking to pull it off. So, I thought it best to start thinking then.

Between the driving, the music and the noise from the back seat, it was a miracle that I didn't have a headache.

I had been driving for well over an hour when the Stony Brook exit loomed before us. The time—and the booze and the food—had done nothing to tame Spike and A.J. They were as goofy as they were at the outset. But as soon as I was on my home turf, I started to feel better.

I knew the Redfern was just a few miles away. I knew I could get rid of Spike once we got there. I knew that right after that, I'd call my dad and get him to pick us up. I saw the light at the end of the tunnel. With luck we were going to get out of this one.

It happened about a block away from the Redfern. My driving that night had been perfect. But when I saw the Redfern just up ahead, I got cocky and too eager. I stopped late and harshly for a STOP sign, then pulled out with a jerk before waiting long enough. We were almost right in front of the Redfern—if he wanted, Spike could've thrown a bottle at *its* window—when I saw the flashing red lights behind us. The siren came next.

I pulled over to the curb. The flashing lights stopped right behind me and I heard the police car door close.

Believe it or not, I think that was the first instant that Spike and A.J. realized that the police had pulled us over.

A.J. sat up real straight and looked at the lights through the back window. He burped again; a burp that rumbled the car.

Spike sat up and looked out the window too.

I saw the shadow of the approaching policeman in the side view mirror.

At that instant, A.J. decides to be sick. He turns to Spike and pukes. And not just pukes. He *projectile vomits*. It was like a high-pressure hose was aimed at Spike and drenched him in Technicolor goo. Everything—boilermakers, beer, mussels, pasta, calzones, tiramisu, chips and then even more beer—squeezed out of A.J. and showered Spike in a near endless spray of barf.

Spike was swimming in A.J.'s puke. He managed to choke out, "Jesus! What the hell's wrong with you!"

"Spike," I said, looking in the rearview mirror. "You make him sick."

It was then the policeman knocked on my window with his billy club.

And from there on, things only got worse.

Chapter Seven

So, we went to jail.

It's hard for me to tell you about it because there wasn't a moment of it that wasn't awful. And I mean...*awful*. But, here goes.

When I lowered the window after the officer tapped on it, the smell of puke hit the cool spring air like a nuclear explosion. The officer stepped back with all the force of a guy who was pushed. He then took a breath, came closer and said, "Please exit the vehicle."

Spike came out, swiping puke from his clothes with the knife-side of his hand. A.J. staggered out and leaned against the car. He burped and I feared the worst. But he was done. If he was going to throw up any more, he would have to heave up a lung. Or maybe an intestine.

I stepped out. The police examined my permit and the next thing we knew, the three of us were being handcuffed and led to the police car.

"Waitaaminute!" Spike roared. "Do you know who I am?"

He turned to me. With my hands cuffed behind my back and being led to a police car, my enthusiasm waned.

"This is Jayson Tuttman," I said, like I was reciting something stupid I learned in third grade. "Spike. The Emperor of First Base."

The officer guiding Spike into the backseat just nodded his head. For all I knew, every night he arrested someone who claimed to be famous.

We were separated at the police station. They led Spike, still protesting, down a long corridor, and me and A.J. to this big cage.

It was weird. It wasn't a jail cell like you saw on television. It was more like a giant chicken coup, made of heavy criss-crossed wire, with a door and simple lock. As he opened the door, the cop asked A.J. if he was okay. A.J. nodded and led me into the cage.

The door closed behind us and the cop walked away.

A.J. was right there with me, but I had never felt more alone in my life.

There was a bench bolted into the wall and A.J. sat silently on it. I stood, looking out in the larger room beyond. It was empty and the door in the distance was shut.

Finally, A.J. muttered something.

"What?" I asked.

"Sorry," he repeated.

"Well that's just wonderful," I said. "As I spend the next twenty years wearing stripes and breaking rocks on the side of the road, I can always tell myself, *at least A.J. was sorry.*"

That did it. A.J. put his face in his hands and started crying.

I stood there, back to him. *Let the jerk cry*, I thought. *Serves him right.*

And then.

Well, and then I shrugged and sat beside A.J. I put my arm around his shoulder and told him he could cry all he wanted.

We were there maybe an hour before the officer returned and unlocked the gate. "On your feet," he said.

A.J. got up and started tucking his shirt back into his pants. I took a breath.

"C'mon," the cop said.

"Can't I make a phone call?" I asked, following him. "I'm supposed to be allowed to make a phone call."

We went through the door and were led down a long corridor. The officer opened another door leading into a room with a metal table and a bunch of folding chairs. "Wait here."

We went in and the door closed. I heard it lock behind him.

A.J. and I looked at one another. "Don't say anything," I said, "until I talk to Dad. He'll know what to do."

Then the door opened and a man in a business suit entered. He was a little guy, maybe thirty pounds heavier than he should've been, with a very tired look about him. I thought that he looked like I felt, but kept my mouth shut.

To my surprise, he held out his hand. "Hi, boys. My name is Bob Steppinitis."

I don't know about A.J., but my eyes got wider. "Steppinitis! You mean, Spike's keeper."

He nodded. No wonder he looked tired. "Look, you kids aren't in any trouble. I already talked to the judge and your parents. They should be here in a minute."

"Our parents," A.J. said. He sounded very afraid.

"Yeah," Steppinitis said. "Not to worry. I told them if there are any legal fees or court dates, we'll cover the costs."

This was too much for me and I had to sit down. I pulled out a folding chair and plopped into it. Steppinitis patted me on the shoulder. I had the feeling he probably had to do that to a lot of people who crossed paths with Spike.

Then the door opened and it was Mr. Lopez. He had a windbreaker over a denim shirt, and dark slacks. I had never seen him standing taller or his face stonier. He just walked in, saying nothing, and glared at A.J. Then he glared at me. He was an equal opportunity glarer.

"Thanks for being so understanding, Mr. Lopez," Steppinitis said. "I was just explaining to the boys that everything will be alright."

Mr. Lopez was about to say something when the door opened again. It was my dad. He had on a light-colored cardigan and his usual khakis. He pushed past everyone and wrapped his arms around me.

I hugged him back.

Then he stepped back and looked at me. "You're dead."

"I know."

"No," he said. "I mean it. You're dead."

"I can explain everything."

"This can all wait," Steppinitis said. "We should meet tomorrow just to smooth over any next steps." He gave a half-smile. "It's all arranged and, with luck, we'll keep it out of the news."

I don't know why, but I had the feeling that Steppinitis had spent the last hour making promises, talking to lawyers, and paying bribes. No wonder Spike relied on him.

And speaking of Spike, the man of the hour chose that moment to come in.

I don't know how, but somehow he had managed to towel away most of A.J.'s puke. He changed his clothes, too. He was now in a gray sweat suit and a pair of sandals. As he walked into the room, the sandals slapped the bottoms of his feet.

The door closed behind him and he scoped out the room like a guy looking for a party. When his eyes settled on Mr. Lopez, he broke out with a dopey grin.

"You must be this young man's dad," he said, putting out his hand.

Mr. Lopez looked at the hand uncertainly.

"Let me tell you, you got a fine boy there," said Spike. "A *fine* boy. Wouldn't be surprised if he ends up in the Major Leagues. That's right, the Major Leagues."

Mr. Lopez smiled and took the hand.

Spike leaned in, all conspiratorial. "Sorry about all the fuss, champ," said he. "Boys night out. You know."

Mr. Lopez nods, smiling and pumping Spike's hand.

Spike figured he had oozed enough charm and took his hand back. His eyes landed on my dad. He turned to Steppinitis and asked, "What's that?"

Steppinitis leans in, all conspiratorial himself. "That's Thom's father."

"No kiddin'?" Spike said. He breaks out into a grin and steps forward, hand out. "Hey, Mr. – ah, Thom's father. No hard feelings, right?"

Now, we all saw it, but it happened so fast we could never swear that we actually *saw* it to remember, if you know what I mean. Sometimes things happen and you can play them back in your memory in slow motion. But this? We could never say that we saw it to remember, though we were there.

My dad returns the smile to Spike, then reaches around his back, like he's taking something out of his back pocket. Then his fist cleaves through the air in a roundhouse punch that would have dropped a moose. His fist smacks against Spike's jaw—*crack!* the sound went, like a bat hitting a baseball—and the next thing you know, Spike is spiraling backward into a mess of folding chairs and is on his ass.

The moment was ruined somewhat when my dad shook his hand and shouted *damn!* at the pain, but I think everyone conceded that the point was his.

Spike sat up among the collapsed chairs, a thin trickle of blood dripping from a gash he got in his hairline going down. He said several words I won't share with you here and started to his feet, murder in his eyes.

Steppinitis jumped forward and put his hands on Spike's shoulders. "Easy."

I don't know what would've happened next, but a policeman entered at all the noise and stood at the door. "What happened?"

"Nothing," Steppinitis said, all easy smiles. "Spike here was just showing them his swing and he slipped into the chairs." He turned to Spike. "Isn't that right...Champ?"

Spike smiled sickly. "Yeah."

The cop looked at us all suspicious, then shrugged and closed the door.

Spike turned to Steppinitis. "I'm goin' to kill that peckerhead," he said, pointing at my old man.

"Spike," Steppinitis said as if butter wouldn't melt in his mouth. "We just managed to avoid arrest for you and a lot of trouble for these kids. Don't make it worse." He took a handkerchief from his jacket pocket and handed it to the ball player. "Clean yourself up and don't make a bigger ass out of yourself than you have already."

Needless to say, I was looking at all of this with a great deal of interest. But to me the most interesting thing was Mr. Lopez. When he got over the initial shock of seeing my dad go all Han Solo on Spike, he started looking like maybe he was the odd man out.

Spike took the handkerchief and marched out of the room. And, outside of seeing snippets of him on television while changing channels, we never saw him again.

Steppinitis was right about many things, but he sure wasn't when it came to the news.

Spike left the police station before we did. Our dads signed what seemed like an endless number of papers and it was very late at night by the time we were let go.

Our dads stepped out of the police station first, but it all happened too fast for them to do anything about it. Because just as A.J. and I stepped over the threshold, we were blinded by the cameras.

A.J. staggered a little at the first *pop* of flashing lights and bumped into me. We were side-by-side for a few seconds as the photographers took pictures, then we separated.

I remember A.J. shading his eyes with his hand and his dad taking him by the elbow. I squinted and stood close to my dad.

"Boys!" one of the photographers said. "Look at the camera!"

Instead, I lowered my head, the way I saw criminals do on TV when they didn't want the press to take photos.

"Tell us about your night out on the town with Spike!" another newsie yelled.

Dad was leading me to the car, and the photographers followed us like coyotes after an injured raccoon. I caught Mr. Lopez giving one photographer the hairy eyeball – and I was afraid he was going to belt him, if for no other reason than to let my dad know he was macho too. But nothing happened.

Dad led me to the car and I hopped in the passenger seat. I slammed the door, pretty close to one of the reporters, and wouldn't have minded at all if I took his finger with me as a souvenir. The flashing lights kept popping as the photographers kept snapping, and I turned my head away from the window.

"We'll be home soon," Dad said, and I think those few moments outside the police station were the worst part of the whole thing for him.

We didn't talk much on the way home. I could tell that he had hurt his hand—it was all swollen and red—and he was mad at me and mad at himself for losing his temper. Every time I started to say something, he cut me off with, "Thomas, I don't want to discuss it."

We pulled into the driveway at home. It was now going on two in the morning, but Mom and Nancy were both awake when I walked in. They were sitting on the couch and watched silently as I marched through the house and walked up the stairs. I was nearly at the top when I heard my dad say, "And don't leave your room until I say so."

My impulse was to slam my door, but I didn't want to make things worse. Instead, I closed it quietly and turned on the light.

For some reason, after all that happened that night, my room looked like an alien landscape. More Middle-earth than Stony Brook. I used the toe of each foot to pull off my shoes and, standing there in my socks, my eyes landed on the poster of Spike over my bed.

I don't know what happened. It started with a rush to jump on the bed and pull down the poster. I did—thumbtacks flying. I then started ripping it to shreds, pulling larger pieces into smaller pieces, and tearing smaller pieces into microscopic bits. And then…I lost it.

I jumped off my bed and kicked over my desk chair. I flung the books off my desk, picked up my PlayStation and threw it across the room. I took my Mets Yearbook and tore out all the pages, actually spitting on the pages with pictures of Spike.

And then, I sat down and cried. I cried like I hadn't since I was a little kid.

I got tired of that after an hour, got undressed and climbed into bed. I thought I wouldn't fall asleep—I was sure I would never, ever sleep again—and in minutes, I was gone.

I don't know how long I was out, but it was a long time. I woke up to find the sun high in the distance. I hadn't set my alarm and no one woke me for school.

I crept out of bed and saw that it was going on noon. I padded to the bedroom door and opened it slightly.

Mom was out there, putting some towels in the linen closet. She turned when she heard the door.

I looked at her. Finally I said, "Hi."

"Hi."

"I missed school." It was the only thing I could think of saying.

"I called in sick for you."

I let that sink in. When it registered, I just looked at her. Her face was tired. And for the first time ever, she looked older.

"Mom," I started.

"Shower and dress," she said. "We're waiting downstairs for you."

We're waiting downstairs for you. Sounds like something they said before a beheading. Or maybe a crucifixion.

I was going to ask which it was, but before I could say a word, she was already heading downstairs.

I took a long time brushing my teeth and then showering and dressing. I was glad that Nancy would be at school, as whatever happened would be embarrassing enough without her watching.

But what I couldn't shake was the feeling of...*dread*. I didn't know what I was going to face down there, but I felt that this was one of those things that changes everything else forever. I wondered if my parents would still love me, and if I would be able to make them understand why I did everything I did. And even if I could make them understand, would they care? And those thoughts just clogged me up so it was hard to breathe.

Finally dressed I went downstairs.

The living room was quiet. I could actually hear the clock on the mantel ticking. Not a good sign.

I went to the kitchen, but that was empty, too.

Then I heard Dad say "in here", and I knew that they were waiting in his study.

I came in. Dad was sitting at his drawing table, an ACE bandage wrapped tightly around his right hand. Mom sat in the armchair nearby, arms folded. If this jury was going to be as merciful as it looked, I was doomed.

"Sit down," Dad said.

I took the third chair in the room and sat. My first impulse was to cry, but I held it back. Instead, I chewed on my inner cheek and waited.

"Sweetheart," Mom opened. I wondered if that was a good sign. "Sweetheart, I'm sure you know that we're very disappointed in you."

I nodded, hanging my head low. I started at the carpet.

Dad didn't say anything. That was bad.

"But we wanted to talk to you before we figured out what to do next."

I nodded, still staring at the carpet.

"So?" she asked.

I looked up.

"So?" I asked.

"Tell us what happened."

"The truth, now," Dad added.

I gulped. And then, taking a deep breath, I told them *everything* that happened that night. *Everything*. Waiting in the lobby, helping Spike out the window, the trip to New York, the boilermakers and the beer and the barfing in the john. I told them all about Samwise Gamgee, and how he would look after Frodo, and if I was worthy of being a citizen of Middle-earth, I had to be there for A.J. too.

I told them about pretending to be a waiter, about Spike throwing the bottle at the window, running to another bar, and the garage attendant suggesting that I drive us all home. I finished with A.J. puking on Spike and the police.

And then...I was done. I don't know how I got it all out. I told it fast and I stumbled a lot, but I said my piece.

And then...silence. I could hear the damn clock ticking in the living room. Then, Dad got up and stood over me. I flinched a little, expecting a smack.

Instead, he leaned over and kissed me on the top of my head. Right there, where I part my hair. And without another word, he just left.

My mother, well...she's different. After a time she reached behind her chair and pulled out my single-volume edition of *Lord of the Rings*.

"You left this out back again."

"Sorry."

She opened it up, paging through it randomly. "You know, Thom, I always encouraged you to read this."

"Yes."

"You know I read it when I was in college?"

"You did?"

She nodded. "It's all about becoming an adult. You have to leave home and make your way in a world that isn't always kind and isn't always just. But Frodo and Samwise know that they have to have a moral center if they're going to make it out of the adventure alive."

"Yes." Elvish is cool, too, but I didn't think now was the time to bring it up.

"The thing that always got me about the story was this: Frodo goes through all of those horrible places, like battlefields, slowly losing everything. His dignity. His self-composure. Even one of his fingers at Mount Doom. But when he's done and survived, he has learned kindness and mercy."

I went back to looking at the carpet.

"I always hoped you'd be a priest some day."

"Mom…"

"But if you're not going to be a priest," she said, paying no attention, "I'd be almost as proud if you became Samwise Gamgee."

That hung in the air for a moment.

"Then…" I hesitated. "Then, I'm not grounded?"

"Oh, no," she said. "You're grounded for life. Maybe longer."

"But—"

"Oh, I'm very proud of you," she said. "More proud at this moment than I ever was before." She shook her head, thinking. "But you're still an idiot. Sorry. Grounded."

I nodded.

"I'd probably lay low around the house for a couple of days," she added. "Why press your luck? Also, keep away from A.J. for now. I heard your dad on the phone with his dad this morning, and it was getting pretty twisted."

"Yes."

"Scat," she said, getting up. "Text one of your friends and find out what the homework is. You're back in school tomorrow."

I sighed. Wow. At least it didn't get any worse.

That was the moment Dad picked to return. He looked a little dicey.

Mom narrowed her eyes. "What is it?"

"I hadn't gone out all day," Dad said, "so I just noticed this. It was on the porch."

He held up the local paper.

"It seems you're famous," he said.

Chapter Eight

So, it got worse.

I took the newspaper from Dad's hand and opened it up. There, in letters two inches high, I saw:

SPIKED!
AREA TEENS ARRESTED AFTER PARTYING WITH MAJOR LEAGUE BAD BOY

Stony Brook residents A.J. Lopez and Thom Wilcox left the police station last night following their arrest with Jayson (Spike) Tuttman, First Baseman of the New York Mets. The trio returned to Stony Brook following a late-night rampage through New York nightspots. The boys, currently juniors at St. Benedict's High School, will meet with Superior Court Judge Alyssa Kroenig in the coming weeks to determine whether charges will be filed. Tuttman, visiting Long Island for a promotional event, was unavailable for comment.

If that wasn't bad enough, right there on the front page was our picture. Somehow, the photographer had managed to miss both of our dads, but there were me and A.J., pale and frightened, looking like deer caught in the headlights.

The photographer snapped us just as we had bumped into one-another, close enough to look like a two-headed man.

But the worst of it all was something I noticed, but I think (I think!) my parents missed: there, near the bottom of the photo, it was clear that A.J. and I were holding hands.

It must've happened just for that instant when we connected, I didn't even realize that we had grabbed hands. I'm not sure even A.J. realized it. But, there it was, on the front page for the whole world to see.

I suddenly felt very dizzy and a little sick.

I felt the newspaper fall from my hand and the room spin. I reached out for the arm of my chair and sank into it.

Mom and Dad were up and around me in minutes.

"Get him a glass of water," Dad said. I was vaguely aware of Mom rushing out of the room.

Dad was rubbing one of my hands to get the blood flowing.

"Thom," he said. "Thom. Don't worry. It's just the local paper. This will all blow over in a couple of days."

Right there on the front page, I thought. *On the front page!*
Faggot, Dillworth said.

Didn't they notice? I wondered. *Were they blind?*

Mom came back with a Coke. "Drink this," she said. "You need the sugar."

I took the glass with shaky hands. The bubbles and cool wetness helped, but I still felt faint.

Did Mr. Lopez notice? I wondered. *Did A.J. even notice?*

I picked up the paper and looked again.

It was something you really had to look for to notice. The photo ended around the level of our knees, and maybe it looked like our hands had just brushed against each other. But me, who knew how connected we were all our lives, I could tell that we were holding hands. Could anyone else?

"Sweetheart," Mom said. "Do you need to lie down?"

I had never felt so disconnected from these two people, who loved me more than anyone else, than I did now. How could I tell them what I saw?

"Yes," I said. "I need to lie down."

"Want to go to the hospital?" Dad asked.

I ran a hand over my forehead. "I'm good," I said. "Just need rest."

I lurched out of the chair and started for my bedroom. At the base of the stairs, Dad stopped me. He settled his good hand over mine on the newel post.

"You're not worrying about college, are you son?" he asked. "This'll all be history in just a few days."

I nodded, saying nothing. It was only in my room that I realized I was still holding the newspaper. I fell into bed looking at it again.

Yes. Holding hands.

I sighed and dropped it onto the floor. I had made a mess of everything.

My phone was on my night table. I was terrified to turn it on—it would only take one eagle-eye in school to notice and people would start talking. If I didn't turn it on, I was safe for now. But…I had to know.

I turned on my phone. I put it on my table and waited for it to fully power up. And when it vibrated with text messages, I looked at it like a Federation starship looking at a Klingon warbird.

I turned away from it and went to my window.

Across from me, A.J.'s window was closed and his shade drawn. I had never seen that before. I wondered what was going on at *his* house.

I went back to my phone and punched in my security code.

I had texts, all right. Dozens of them. *Hundreds of them.* I think every kid I knew in school had texted me—even guys I hardly knew at all.

I quickly started scanning through them. Most were brief and they were all surprisingly alike:

Hey, playboy.

why didn't you take me?

so now you're famous.

what is spike like?

guess who we're talking about?

put this on your college application!

can you get me to meet spike?

I read one after another after another after another. No one noticed it, I think. No one knew I was holding A.J.'s hand—I was safe.

I was halfway through them all, answering none, when I noticed that I had nothing from A.J. No text, no email, no voicemail, not a single word.

The only message that wasn't stupid came from Preston (Big surprise). He asked, **Are you ok?**

I answered him. **Grounded, but alive.**

I held the phone close to me, waiting for a return note.

When are you coming back to school?

Tomorrow, I wrote.

Nothing.

I waited.

And waited.

If people were saying anything, I'm sure Preston would've heard. But he said nothing. Unable to wait any more, I texted, **Anything I should know?**

He buzzed back, COUNTLESS THINGS.

He picks *now* to be funny.

I went for the direct approach. WHAT ARE PEOPLE SAYING?

After what seemed like forever, he texted, LOTS OF THEM WISH IT WAS THEM INSTEAD OF YOU.

I put the phone down and felt my body tremble with relief.

AND I THINK THE SCHOOL WANTS TO MEET WITH YOUR PARENTS, came next. But *that* I could live with.

I texted A.J. next. WHAT'S GOING ON WITH YOU?

No answer.

I waited again.

And waited. And waited.

And waited.

After twenty minutes, I figured A.J. was radio silent for the duration. I'd have to talk to him tomorrow.

I texted Preston, SEE YOU TOMORROW.

Then, on impulse, I added, YOU'RE A GOOD FRIEND.

Preston, ever literal, answered with the truth. YES. I KNOW.

Somehow, that made me feel that things were on the right track. I put my head down on the pillows and looked at my ceiling. I hadn't been up for more than an hour or so, but the next thing I knew…I was fast asleep.

When Mom was shaking me awake, I blinked and checked the window. The light was low and it was late afternoon. I looked up at her in alarm.

"Everything's okay," she said. "Wash up for dinner."

I was running a hand through my hair as I watched her leave my room. I quickly brushed my teeth and hair and went down.

I was just about beginning to think it was all over. My parents didn't mention it much during dinner, and my nerves over the front page photo were finally settling down. I expected Mr. Lopez to come knocking on the door at any minute, but things were quiet.

Mom drove me to school the next day. There was no talk of me and A.J. traveling together. I thought it best to keep quiet for once. As I was walking into the school, guys I had never even spoken to waved at me. And as I made it to my locker, some even patted me on the back.

I didn't get it. I was in big trouble, I found out my idol was a world-class jerk, and everyone thought I was some kind of hero. Go figure.

I saw A.J. standing near his locker with about five guys hanging on his every word. I grabbed books from my locker and came over. The other guys all patted me on the back and A.J. put out his fist so I could bump it.

Now…we've been friends all our lives, and I had never seen him fist bump anyone. To me, it's the kind of thing you do to people you pretend are your friends, but are not really friends. But I didn't say anything.

"I saw you in the paper," one of the guys said.

I swallowed hard.

"Yeah?"

"Cool," he said.

"Yeah," I agreed. "Cool."

The bell rang. Homeroom was beginning.

"Hey, A.J.," I said. "I need to talk to you."

"Later, little bud," he said. And then he fist bumped me again.

Later little bud...? And...*another fist bump?*

I went through the rest of the day in a kind of haze. I had never been more popular, but the one person I was closest to ignored me. I couldn't understand. Was he mad about everything that happened with Spike? Was he embarrassed? Did his dad tell him to keep away from me (That's the option I liked the best)?

I wasn't able to catch up with A.J. until school was letting out. He was just walking through the door when I caught sight of him and raced over to catch up.

"A.J.!"

He turned.

Now that I caught up to him, I didn't know what to say. His face was as dark and handsome as ever, but something was missing. He looked at me.

"So," I said.

He stood there.

"So," I tried again.

"Yeah?"

"So," I figured three times was a charm, "what happened? Did you get in trouble?"

He shrugged. "They're still figuring out what they are going to do."

He looked over his shoulder.

"Want to get together later tonight?"

He turned back to me. "There's my ride," he said. "Maybe later."

And he fist bumped me again.

I watched A.J. as he ran down the stairs to a car with a bunch of other guys I saw around the school, but didn't know well. Except for one.

Robert Dillworth.

He was there, in the back seat, with the other guys.

Faggot, Robert Dillworth said

I was watching the car grow small in the distance while it drove away when Preston's voice startled me.

"You appear to have recovered," he said.

It was so unexpected, I nearly jumped out of my skin.

"Do I?" I asked.

Mom was coming to pick me up and I saw our car in the distance. "You need a lift?" I asked.

"No, thanks," he said. I could feel his eyes on me.

"What?"

"It'll be alright," he said.

The car pulled to the curb and I started for it. I didn't even turn to him when I said, "Thanks."

"I'll try and see you later," I heard him say as I closed the car door on him.

I spent most of the afternoon in my room, looking at the blank spot on my wall where the Spike poster used to be, and trying to get lost in a copy of *Dune*. Things were quiet and I could feel the hours drip slowly away…it must be what it's like to watch the polar ice caps melt.

I still had nearly an hour before dinner so I got up and stretched. I went to my window and I could see that A.J. had his blinds drawn. I saw that the family car was there – but I didn't know if A.J.'s new best friends had dropped him off yet.

There was still daylight, so I checked that our block was empty and stepped out onto the tree. I made great time through the branches and in seconds was outside of his window. I had just slipped a leg over the sill when I heard voices.

A.J. pulled up the blinds as I was stepping in. The room was filled with other guys—the crowd that he had driven away with, including Dillworth. A.J. blinked and said, "Dude," and then fist-bumped me.

I half-heartedly returned the bump. A.J. had his stereo on—though he was never into music before—and the other guys were slumped around the floor, the bed and his desk.

"You always come in through the window?" Dillworth asked.

"That's Thom, for you," A.J. said, turning to him. "He's great at planning. If it wasn't for him, I wouldn't ever have had a chance to make friends with Spike."

Dillworth kept his eyes on me and if anyone could ever say *I hate your guts* without moving his lips, it was him.

Unlike me, A.J. kept all the photos of Spike up in his room. Some of the guys had cans of soda, a couple others were paging through his Mets Yearbook.

"So," Dillworth said. "What do *you* want?"

"I'm here to see *my* friend," and as soon as it came out of my mouth, I saw that I had somehow embarrassed A.J.

"Wassup?" A.J. said. Something else I never heard him say before.

Put on the spot, I realized I didn't have anything to say. "I was just wondering if the school set up a meeting with your folks."

"Yeah," A.J. said, and smiled at the guys. "No big deal."

I thought it was a big deal, but kept my mouth shut. "Are we going together?"

"Don't know," he said. "I have to ask my folks."

Long pause.

"Oh," I said.

"Well," I said.

"Yeah," A.J. said.

The other guys were all looking at me.

"Well," I said again—I'm nothing if not predictable—"I'll head off."

I started to climb out of the window. As soon as I stepped onto the branch, A.J. closed the blinds. Just as they touched the sash, I heard Dillworth say, "That guy's a little faggot."

It was stupid and it would only bring even more trouble on us, but, boy, I got mad. I turned and was through the window so quick, I pulled the blinds out of the wall. They fell to the floor with a crash and I hopped over them, arms out, reaching for Dillworth.

He was standing by the desk and I slammed into him like a truck. We spilled onto the floor and I was grabbing at him while he had a tight grip on my wrists. One of the kids started shouting—what, I had no idea—and we rolled around the room for a moment.

Dillworth tried to bring up his knee, but we were too close and all he did was get his thigh between my legs. I wanted to head butt him, but the best I did was knock my forehead against his jaw. I heard his teeth snap against each other as a bolt of pain lit up my scalp.

I don't know what would've happened next, but then A.J. had his hands on my shirt collar and two other kids grabbed Dillworth by the elbows. I tried to pull away from A.J. for another tussle when the bedroom door opened so hard and so fast, it slammed against the wall.

It was Mr. Lopez. He filled the doorway like an angry god and one look told me he was out for blood. I felt all the fight go out of me.

"What's going on here?"

"That little jerk started a fight," Dillworth said.

Mr. Lopez turned to A.J.

"Not exactly," A.J. said. "You see—"

Mr. Lopez didn't give him time to finish. He pointed a finger at me. "I'm sick and tired of you. You got my son in a lot of trouble and you're a bad influence on him. I never want to see you in my house again. Understand?"

"But—"

"*GET OUT!*"

I didn't say anything more. I could feel the eyes of everyone on me. I didn't even go towards the door. I just turned and climbed through the window. I heard it slam shut behind me.

I was shaking by the time I got to my own window. I stepped inside and there was Preston, sitting on the floor with his back against my bed. My mother had just let him into my room again.

"I didn't know what to expect," he said, "but coming through the window *is* a surprise."

I don't know what my expression was, but my face felt hot.

He looked at me through those thick glasses. "Are you okay?"

"Yes," I said, though my answer sounded a little strangled.

I went to my desk and sat. Preston's eyes followed me. I never knew what he was thinking, but I always had the weird feeling that he knew what *I* was thinking. At any rate, he didn't say anything.

I don't know how long we sat there, not talking. Finally, he said, "You want to PlayStation?"

I swallowed and nodded yes. I sank to the floor next to him and we started to play.

I waited while Preston mastered the console. He was dressed in his usual black jeans and dark blue pullover. He always looked one second away from being beamed aboard the *Enterprise*. I could see the game lights reflected on the surface of his glasses.

In a goofy kinda way, he was really cute. I was beginning to think that maybe *he* was my best friend.

Without thinking, I put my hand on his thigh.

If he even noticed, I have no idea. He was so intent on the game, Martians could've landed outside without him noticing (Okay—*that* he would've noticed). Every time he scored, I gave his leg a squeeze.

The heat generated by his body came through the black denim and my hand grew warmer.

174

After forever, he got knocked out of the game. I hadn't looked at the screen at all, just at him as he played. When he turned to hand me the console, his face was very close to mine.

I don't know what happened—I sure as hell didn't plan on it – but when he turned toward me I leaned over and kissed him.

That got his attention. He looked at me, more shocked than embarrassed or angry, and noticed my hand on his thigh for the first time. With a little half smile he gently patted my hand and then lifted it, placing it on my lap.

"Thanks," he said, voice low. "But I gotta get home."

He put down the console and got to his feet.

I jumped up. "Wait a minute! Preston—I can explain!"

But he just patted me on the shoulder, like I was a cadet who had somehow just flunked out of Starfleet, and went for the door.

I followed him to the door and when he opened it, I asked, "Friends?" I might have sounded a little desperate.

"Always," he said, and went off to Ceti Alpha VI, or wherever it was he vanished to. But when the door closed, it had an awful final sound to it.

I looked at the clock—it was getting near dinnertime. In less than a day, I managed to screw up my two closest friendships. And if Preston behaved in any way other than the interstellar Vulcan diplomat I knew him to be, I wouldn't *need* to have my picture on the front page holding hands with A.J.

Preston could tell them.

Sometimes, it feels like secrets are all you have. And once they can be taken away from you, it gets awfully lonely.

***

The next few weeks, A.J. spent a lot of time with Dillworth and that gang. We would nod and wave and smile and fist bump (fist bump?), but there was a distance there that we never had before. In all our lives, it was the most we had ever been apart.

And every day it made me a little sadder.

When A.J. and Dillworth were hanging out (or, worse still, that whole group I had met in his room), it was pretty clear to me I wasn't welcome. I didn't want to come out and ask A.J. why he was acting so different, mainly because I thought it would make him wonder…Wonder, *what?* I wondered. How I defined our friendship? How *he* defined it? It seemed like it would open more questions than I wanted to answer at that moment.

But A.J. and those guys were all over the halls at school, and somehow I was not.

I was afraid that I had messed up my friendship with Preston, but he never said anything, and neither did I.

When he came over for PlayStation he sat just where he always did and never seemed ill at ease. If anything, *I* was ill at ease. I kept trying to act cool instead of just being myself.

My parents and I had a meeting with the principal at school, and after a great deal of explaining, it seemed that I was not going to be in trouble. At least, not too much trouble. Dad made it clear that what happened after school hours and outside of school grounds was our business and not the school's, and if they wanted to take issue with that, they could talk to our lawyer. The principal insisted that I go to counseling with one of the Christian Brothers at the school once a week, and Dad consented to that. *For now*, he added. Getting out of a different class once a week to meet with a counselor made me feel awkward and somehow defective. I don't know if A.J. had to do the same, we never compared notes.

I never told my parents about Mr. Lopez or seeing less of A.J., but they knew something was up. At least Mom did – she always made a point of asking after him and wondering if we would get back to driving each other to school. I would just smile embarrassedly and mumble something like *soon* and change the subject.

So it was several weeks since I had really spent time with A.J. when we were scheduled to go to court.

Steppinitis had been in touch with Dad and had even arranged for a lawyer to come with us. The lawyer, a severe-looking middle aged woman with her hair tightly pulled back, was named Nguyen and she looked at me through little half-moon shaped glasses. She came to our house one evening for the initial meeting, and Mom and Dad sat with me in the study while I went over the whole story again with her.

She nodded, saying nothing, keeping notes. Finally she said, "That tallies with what Mr. Lopez said."

"A.J.'s dad?" I asked. For some reason, I got nervous.

"No, young Mr. Lopez," she said.

"So, what do we do?" Dad asked.

Ms. Nguyen put her moon glasses on the desk. "The district attorney is considering pressing child endangerment charges against Mr. Tuttman."

Spike, I thought, almost smiling. *The Emperor of First Base*.

"What does that mean for us?"

She shrugged. "Nothing." She turned to me. "When we meet with the judge, keep quiet, answer questions exactly as they're asked and don't add anything to your answers. And we should be fine."

She started piling files into her leather briefcase. "Juvenile court's a funny thing," she said, though no one was laughing. "It's not really court the way you understand it. It's more like a structured discussion before the State decides on next steps, if any. The trick here is for them to decide that they don't need to take any." She looked up at me. "Got that?"

"Yes, ma'am," I said.

"You seem like good kids," she said. "I want to keep it that way. And if you come out of it in one piece, then it's unlikely that they will prosecute Mr. Tuttman."

"I wish they would," Mom said.

"Think twice about that," Ms. Nguyen said. "That would keep this whole thing alive and in the public eye. And it would keep Thom here involved. No, the best thing for everybody is for this to just go away."

The court date came and both families went to the county court house in separate cars.

Both sets of parents were in attendance, and Nguyen and Steppinitis met us in the lobby. Mr. Lopez met him warmly, while Mom and Mrs. Lopez retreated towards the door to talk in whispers. Dad stayed with me and A.J.

He put a hand on each of our shoulders. "Don't worry, guys. It'll be okay."

I realized that people only said things would be okay when there was a real possibility that they wouldn't be okay. I nodded to him and smiled weakly at A.J.

It had been so many weeks since we had really spoken, that he now seemed like someone I barely knew. And somehow that made me sadder than the whole court date situation.

We were ushered upstairs to the judge's private chambers, and when the clerk opened the double doors to let us in, I felt like reaching out and taking A.J.'s hand again. But I didn't dare.

Steppinitis was told to wait outside. We all took seats around the judge's desk, and I watched as Nguyen took a sheaf of papers from her satchel.

Judge Kroenig was a heavy-set woman in late middle age with gray hair and one wandering eye. It looked like her right eye was boring right into you, while her left was trying to see what was going on in the next room. I heard that justice was blind, but this was ridiculous.

"Judge," Nguyen started.

"One moment, counselor," Judge Kroenig said. "I'm paging through the brief."

We all sat there silently, the only sound in the room the rustling of the pages.

Finally, Judge Kroenig looked up. "Is Mr. Tuttman here today?"

"No, Your Honor," Nguyen said.

"My son has never been in trouble before," Mr. Lopez said.

Kroenig regarded him with her one good eye. "And you are?"

Mr. Lopez patted A.J. on the shoulder. "The boy's father."

She sized him up silently, then went back to the brief. Finally she said, "If the parents would please leave for a moment," she said. "Ms. Nguyen and the boys remain."

"Your Honor!" Dad started up.

She *tut-tutted* him with a motion. "Relax, Mr..." she checked the files, "Mr. Wilcox. Council will be here."

Nguyen nodded to my folks and the four parents got up and went to the door, my mom looking back at me with every step.

"If you please," Kroenig said. "Outside."

Once the door was closed, Judge Kroenig focused her attention on us. "Who wants to go first?"

A.J. and I exchanged terrified looks.

"I'll make it easy," she said. "Did either of you gentlemen know Mr. Tuttman before the night in question?"

"Well, we *heard* of him," A.J. said.

"We were his biggest fans," I said. "We tried to get to all of his games."

"Hmm," Judge Kroenig said. Then she trained her good eye on me. "You. Tell me the whole story, from the beginning. Leave nothing out."

"Your Honor," Nguyen said. "I object. I would rather you ask specific questions."

"I am," Judge Kroenig said. "I'm asking what happened. You...Mr. Wilcox. Start at the beginning."

And so…I did. I told her how A.J. got interested in baseball, and how that interest grew into our liking Spike. I told her about the banners and the letters and even Western Union. Then I told her about the night in New York.

When I finished, she looked at A.J. "Is that correct?"

"No, Your Honor," he said.

I nearly jumped out of my skin.

"It is, too!" I said.

"No, Your Honor," A.J. said. "What Thom isn't telling you, is that I got very drunk that night and he did everything he could to get me home. And he only got caught because I guess he was trying to stay by me to make sure nothing happened." He looked down at the floor, then back at her. "So. I guess I'm trying to say that it's all my fault."

I could hear the clock ticking on the judge's desk. Finally Judge Kroenig exhaled loudly and pointed over her shoulder.

"See that door? That's my private room. Please wait in there while I speak to your parents."

We got up.

"And don't touch anything," she added.

Nguyen was opening the door for our folks just as we were going in the other room. I could see the worry on Mom and Dad's face.

Judge Kroenig's private office contained a simple metal desk, a black office chair, several bookshelves crammed with legal books, a few chairs, a couch, and tons of family pictures. I went to the couch and A.J. sat next to me.

We could hear muffled voices through the door, but couldn't make out the words.

Finally A.J. said, "How do you think it went?"

"I don't know."

"What do you think will happen to us?"

"I don't know."

Silence.

"Thanks for what you said out there," I said.

"It's just the truth."

More silence.

"I haven't been very nice to you lately," he said.

"I hadn't noticed."

"No?"

"No."

Even more silence.

"Sorry 'bout that," he said. "I've been a dick."

"Yes," I said. Well…the truth always seemed to work for Preston.

He turned and looked me in the eye. His eyes were big and brown and somehow liquid. I felt my heart make little jumps in my chest. "You forgive me?"

I thought I wouldn't let him off too easily. I thought I should make him anxious. I thought he should know how annoyed I was. Instead I said, "Okay."

He grinned and we shook hands. No fist bump.

The door opened. It was Nguyen. "You boys can come in."

We got up. We had both worn our Sunday suits, and we both reflexively straightened our ties. He nodded to me as if he was ready and we went in.

We took our seats and the Judge started without any preliminary. "Mr. Lopez and Mr. Wilcox, we will not press charges provided you remain out of trouble for one year, starting today. However, if you appear before this court during that time, we will instigate proceedings against you. Is that clear?"

"Yes, Your Honor," we said in stereo.

"And, if the Court decides at some future date to press charges against Mr. Tuttman, it is understood that you will truthfully testify in the matter. Is that understood?"

A.J. nodded vigorously, but I croaked, "Yes, Your Honor."

"Very well," she said, getting to her feet. "The matter is dismissed. For now."

I don't know about A.J., but I felt like a ten-ton weight had been taken from my chest. When I walked into the lobby, my legs felt a little rubbery.

Steppinitis was there, he whirled round as we stepped out. He and Nguyen exchanged a look and seemed to communicate telepathically (I wondered if either knew Preston).

Steppinitis came forward and shook A.J. by the hand, and then Mr. Lopez. He then handed Mr. Lopez an envelope. He opened it, looked inside, and thanked Steppinitis before taking his hand again.

Steppinitis then went to me and did the same before handing Dad a matching envelope. Dad looked inside and then gave Steppinitis a look that could curdle milk.

"Not enough?" Steppinitis wanted to know.

Dad folded the envelope once and stuffed it in the other man's jacket pocket. He then said something I had never heard Dad say before – even at his angriest. When I got over my shock, he hustled me and Mom out the door, leaving Steppinitis and A.J. and family behind.

I never asked what was in the envelope, but I never figured I had to.

***

So, before you knew it, we were back to crawling through the elm tree to each other's rooms, hanging out with Preston, and me doing track. If Preston ever said anything to A.J. about the night I tried to kiss him, it never got back to me.

185

The first time I was in A.J.'s room after the fight with Dillworth, I noticed his Spike poster was missing also. And the Yearbook never made a return appearance. And once, when I told him I'd see him at the ballgame when I was done with track, what he told me he was, "Through with baseball. For now."

The only relic on display was the newspaper photo of the two of us, and the headline SPIKED!

Instead of baseball, A.J. was spending a lot more time at the school gym. I would run track and come back to St. John's to pick him up after he did a long set of weights and isometric exercises. He told me that I should work out with him, but it always seemed like a much bigger hassle than just running track.

One night near the end of our junior year, I picked up A.J. after school and we headed home. We caught Preston coming out of the library, and he decided to tag along. (We had told Preston all about our adventure with Spike. His one comment was, "Amusing." With friends like him...)

Now that Spike and baseball were out of our lives, we had somehow settled back into *Lord of the Rings* territory. Preston had scored some Blu-rays of old adaptations of the stories, including a cartoon *Hobbit* made for television, and an animated version of the first half of *Lord of Rings* from the eighties.

We were talking about them with the sense of importance that only true fanatics have. We kept it up when we got to A.J.'s house and he asked us in.

We were climbing the stairs to A.J.'s room when his sister Lupe, visiting from grad school, passed us in the hall. Preston caught sight of her and nearly bowed.

I never saw Preston interested in anyone (or anything) like he was interested in Lupe. Maybe it was because she was in graduate school, and Preston thought he would eventually go there himself. At any rate, they started talking and, next thing you know, all four of us were hanging out in A.J.'s room.

We all sat on the floor and talked for nearly forty minutes. Preston and Lupe started out with the idea of global government, with Lupe in favor and Preston picking holes in it. A.J. and I weren't all that interested and they chattered in the background while we pulled out the PlayStation.

Then they were going at gender roles and social constructs. Each was tearing into the thinking of the other, but I had a sense that they were enjoying themselves too. It was like Preston was practicing for the Big Brain Leagues and Lupe was showing him the ropes.

Then it got into "the viability of government-funded space exploration vs. the more entrepreneurial, risk-taking model," as Preston put it. They were really having fun with that one, no matter how many snarky remarks they aimed at one another. Finally, me and A.J. said we had enough and told them to take it to the United Nations.

Lupe smiled and looked at her phone. "Gotta run, anyway," said she. She looked at Preston and added, "Good talking to you." She upped and headed for whatever part of the house budding brainiacs hide in.

"A remarkable and stimulating presence," Preston said once she was gone.

"Does that mean you like her?" A.J. asked.

"Her mind is invigorating."

"I think that means yes," I said.

"Someday," Preston said, eyes serious behind his glasses, "you gentlemen will learn to appreciate intelligent conversation."

"We appreciate intelligent conversation!" we said in unison. It was almost stereo.

Preston simply nodded.

A.J. put down the PlayStation and stretched before sitting on the bed. He looked absently at the blank space where his Spike poster used to be and said, "You know what I just got from eBay?"

"What?"

"A poster from that animated *Lord of the Rings*," he said. "The old one. It's great. C'm'ere."

I got up and we went to his closet. He pulled out a poster tube and gently took this thing out. It was a big poster – the same size you see in movie theater lobbies – and he unrolled it in front of us.

He was right. It was a great poster. It was Gandalf holding this enormous sword and pointing into the distance while the sky overhead swirled with clouds and lightning. At his feet, Frodo and Samwise stood in awe.

Preston whistled. "That *is* a beaut."

A.J. pointed over his bed. "I'm going to put it over there." He rolled it up and put it back in the tube. "I never knew what made us so excited about Spike in the first place."

I shook my head. "Beats me. We musta been crazy."

"Oh, that one is easy," Preston said.

We looked at him. "Yeah?"

"Clearly you are in love with one another," Preston said, like he was explaining that cereal is always better with milk. "But you repressed your feelings for one another because you didn't want to admit them. So you sublimated them into an affection for Spike."

I felt my brows knit. A.J.'s mouth fell open.

Preston's phone *pinged* and he pulled it from his back pocket. He checked his texts and said, "Sorry, guys. Dinner." He got to his feet. "See you tomorrow."

And with that, he left.

A.J. and I looked at one another.

Then I shrugged and he laughed.

"Sometimes," said I, "the brains get in the way of his sanity."

"Damn," A.J. said, putting the poster in the closet.

And then...somehow, Preston ruined the rest of the day. A.J. and I tried PlayStation again, and then we just talked about nothing, but we suddenly felt uncomfortable and uneasy. In about twenty minutes I had picked up my books and told him I'd catch him tomorrow.

As soon as I stepped out of his front door, I felt like I'd had some kind of narrow escape.

That night I didn't say a whole lot at dinner myself. Mom and Nancy seemed to be having a good time talking about

Faggot, Robert Dillworth said.

the day at school. Dad was really pleased with his cartoon that day, because he said the Stony Brook School Board had a black eye coming. I just smiled blandly at most of it and ate silently and deliberately.

After dinner I said I had homework and ran up to my room. I don't know why, but I locked my door. Something I never do. In some weird way, I felt like the world outside was ganging up on me.

I concentrated on homework as best I could, then went and took a shower and brushed my teeth. I yelled my goodnights down the stairs and climbed into bed.

I was reading a Heinlein novel. A good one, *Sixth Column*. But all the words started to jumble on me as I tried to concentrate. So I threw the book on the floor and turned out the light.

I was lying on my back, looking up at the ceiling. The soft glow from the streetlight outside cast a rectangular bar of light up there. I stared at it, willing my brain to be empty.

It was the light that tipped me off.

The light flickered, and then a black bar of shadow slowly rose up through the shaft of light.

Someone was opening my window!

I sat up in bed.

The window now open, A.J. threw a leg over the sill and entered my bedroom.

He was also in his pajamas. His bushy hair was matted down in places and it looked like he was also having trouble sleeping. In the reflected streetlight, he looked impossibly handsome.

"A.J.," I said. Unoriginal and obvious, but the best I could come up with. Suddenly, I felt afraid.

A.J. padded over to my bed and sat down beside me. I sat up more.

A.J. was looking at me. A little scared, I think.

Then, he wrapped his arms around me and brought his lips to mine and we were kissing.

It was, really, my first kiss. And it was the kiss that I would measure every other kiss against for the rest of my life.

Finally, he pulled away and looked at me.

"A.J.," I said.

He looked at me some more, eyes kinda at half mast. He kissed me one more time and said, "Thom. I love you."

Then he turned and raced back to the window like the room was on fire. He closed the window and was gone.

I sat there. In shock. Staring at the window. Still feeling the pressure of his lips against mine. And then I thought, *so this is love.*

Chapter Nine

So, that was the summer A.J. and I fell in love.

Or, maybe it's more correct to say that's the summer A.J. and I realized we were in love. I think maybe we were *always* in love. Maybe we just needed Preston to tell us.

Needless to say, I couldn't sleep that night. I hopped out of bed and watched A.J. crawl through the elm like a panther and enter his own bedroom window. The light went out and I stood there for maybe an hour, just looking at his darkened window.

The next day at school was a little weird, like we were with each other the night before after Preston talked to us. When school was over I ran track, like always, and he went to the school gym. When I went to pick him up, I think he was surprised.

We left school without talking, just walking side-by-side. I was leading the way and took us past our houses and down towards where Preston lived. We passed his house, too, and soon I had taken A.J. to the railroad tracks.

He padded down the tracks, book bag over his shoulder, hands in his pockets. I walked quietly beside him, saying nothing. After a few minutes of this, I saw a clump of trees and said, "C'm'ere."

I led him to the trees and dropped my book bag. He stood there looking at me. Maybe trembling a little.

I reached up and pulled the book bag from his shoulder so it fell next to mine.

I reached out and put my arms around his and held him close to me.

"Oh, A.J.," I said.

We hugged tightly for a few moments (If I hugged him any tighter, I'd be on the other side of him).

Then I looked up. And he made his kissy face.

When A.J. kisses you – not that this is going to happen to you, but just so you know – his eyes sorta halfway close and get dizzy and his lips sorta pucker in the middle. He leaned down and I stood on my toes and we kissed again.

So, not to creep you out, but I was never happier in my life than when I was kissing A.J. We stood there and kissed for a few minutes, only pausing briefly for air.

Then, I think he got spooked by being outdoors and in the daylight and we scooped up our bags and hit the tracks again.

And that was the beginning of our romance. We spent what was left of our junior year making out on the railroad tracks and just being happy with one another. Sometimes, when we were on the tracks, I'd hold hands with him, and that made me feel one hundred feet tall.

We didn't tell anybody. And nobody knew. We were always together already, and now we were still always together. But now, we were always together and in love.

Well, when I say no one knew, there was always Preston. Whenever he wanted to hang out with us, we'd say *we're busy*, and he'd just smile in that infuriating, knowing way of his. One day, I seriously considered talking to him about it. But I was afraid. Not afraid that he'd be freaked out – hell, *he* told us! – but that he would say something that would make it all even more confusing.

So I kept my mouth shut.

But for the first time in my life, I was wondering, *what comes next?* A.J. and I were in love, and I didn't want that to change. If I wasn't only going-on-seventeen, I would've married him in a heartbeat (Funny…Nancy was right all those years ago! I *did* want to marry A.J.!). But that didn't seem like something that could happen now.

With school over, the first priority was to look for a summer job. A.J. told me that he wanted us to find something where we could work together so we wouldn't be apart all day. I thought that was a great idea.

We went to various stores around Stony Brook, looking to see if they could take us on. But we had no takers for us as a duo. We even went to a couple of pizza parlors, but no dice.

A.J. thought GameStop would be a good idea, but, again, nothing for the both of us. I was more interested in us getting a gig at the library or the local Barnes and Noble. But, for some reason, that didn't inspire him.

It was A.J.'s mom who saved the day. She made a few calls to people she knew, and, next thing you know, we're working in one of the cafeterias at Stony Brook University. We were going to start right after Fourth of July weekend to work the summer semester and we couldn't have been happier.

That July fourth, A.J.'s folks had a family barbeque and my family attended. Dad and Mr. Lopez made a big deal about grilling the burgers and hot dogs (what is it about old guys and grilling?), and our moms made everything else. I put away three burgers that night (I seem to be starving all the time) and A.J. matched me burger-for-burger and beat me by one hot dog.

There were fireworks that night and A.J. and I wanted to watch them alone. We told our folks that we were going to goof off with PlayStation and went to A.J.'s room before the fireworks started. When we got there, we kept the lights off and walked to the window. I sorta had my arm around A.J.'s waist and he had an arm around mine. We watched the horizon, waiting for the fireworks to start.

And they did…They shot them off over the State Park as they do every year. I love fireworks. Always have. A.J. likes them, too, but I don't think he ever did as much as I do (Nothing makes me happier than stuff blowing up).

That night, there was a riot of color in the sky. Lights would flash, and we would only feel the concussive *boom* after the sound caught up. Huge blossoms of red, then white, then blue. Great purple blossoms where the sound of the explosion echoed in the heavy night air, silvery things that whizzed high before fizzing out. At last came the big finale, where dozens of explosive lights filled the sky. I loved it, but what I loved most of all was watching it with A.J.'s arm around me.

As the sky lit up in a million colors, I turned over and snatched a kiss from A.J.

Which is when the door opened.

A bolt of light from the hallway cut through A.J.'s darkened bedroom and a shadow stood in the doorway.

"I thought you guys were going to do PlayStation."

It was A.J.'s mom.

We instantly took our arms from around our waists. Actually, we *whipped* them away. *Did she see us kiss?*

"We were just watching the end," A.J. said.

"That's what we were doing," I said. Which, somehow, made it worse.

She looked at us. Was she suspicious? "Great. Have fun." She made a point of turning on the light.

A.J. and I stood there. Then, saying nothing, he took out his PlayStation and put it on the desk. "Let's go back to the barbeque," he said.

"Yeah."

We went back for the ice cream and to listen to our dads tell goofy stories. A.J.'s mom didn't seem to behave any differently towards us. In a weird way, that made me *more* nervous. *Was* she acting differently? Or was she pretending *not* to act differently? Did she see something and didn't care? Did she not see something, so had nothing to care about? Would she care if she did see something?

Stuff like that can keep you awake at night.

The next day was our first day at work. Since we were still a few weeks away from our seventeenth birthday, my mom drove us to Stony Brook University.

As soon as we got out of the car and were walking to the cafeteria, I asked, "Your mom say anything?"

"No," he said. But he seemed stressed.

"Relax," I said. "If she was going to say anything, she would've already."

I hoped.

The first day of any new job is hard, but that day was even harder for me than it had to be. First off, there was all the stress of last night. Second, though he seemed cool, I could tell that A.J. was a little freaked out. And third, well…there was that whole *what comes next?*

Since we were in love, it never dawned on me that we wouldn't be together. But we would have to tell our parents…someday. And when would that be? And how? And how would they take it? And what about college? We had both made tentative plans to go to Stony Brook, but A.J.'s dad had also taken him to see Susquehanna and Syracuse, where he hoped his ball playing would get him a scholarship. And…if A.J. had quit ball for good, what about those scholarships?

So while A.J. and I learned about food handling and plastic gloves and hair nets and no facial hair and not mixing serving spoons because of allergens and one hundred other bits of important info, my head was filled with that whole *what comes next?*

During training, I'd sneak a look at A.J. every now and then. He would catch me at it and smile, but the smile was a little uncomfortable. Like if somebody caught him smiling at me it would somehow be wrong.

The next few days we worked and would spend lunch time together. We'd hold hands under the table, or, sometimes, we'd just put our feet over each other's shoes. Sometimes, we'd just look really closely at each other. That was really easy with A.J., because he had these big brown eyes that it was easy to get lost in.

The first Friday after work, having finished dinner at home, I climbed through the elm to his window. He was at his desk when I scrambled over the window sill. He turned and smiled and I came over to kiss him, but before I got close, he locked his bedroom door. He had never done that before.

And then he kissed me. Then he turned and unlocked the door.

"Why you doing that?"

"'Cause it would freak 'em out if they found it locked," he said. "Why *make* them suspicious?"

I stood on my toes and gave him a quick kiss on the cheek. "Smart." I went and sat on the floor by his bed. "Wanna PlayStation?"

He grabbed his PlayStation and we went at it. We were playing for nearly an hour when his mom opened the door.

"Thom," she said, smiling. "Didn't know you were here."

"Just doin' PlayStation."

There it was again. That…look. Was she…suspicious? Or did I imagine that she was?

"Great," she said. "Don't play too long."

The door closed. A.J. started up again, but I fell silent.

"What?" he asked.

"Well," I said. "Someday we're going to have to tell our folks."

"Why?" He looked at me like I just grew another head.

"Because," I said.

"Because why?"

"Well…because we have to."

"Why?"

"Well…we have to tell them *something*."

"Why?"

"Aren't we going to live together some day?"

"I hope so."

"So, what will we tell them?"

He shrugged. "We'll figure something out then."

"You mean…like I'm just your roommate?"

He shrugged again. "Sure. That sounds good."

He started playing again, but I just stared ahead.

He stopped. "You're unhappy."

"No. I'm not."

"Yes. You are."

"Okay. I am."

"About what?"

Now it was my turn to shrug. "Just wondering."

"About what?"

"About stuff."

He let that sink in. "Preston's got nothing on you."

"What does that mean?"

"I don't understand either of you, but when I don't understand him, at least he's talking some kind of English."

I was quiet a moment longer.

"You ashamed of me?"

"Never."

Finally, I picked up the PlayStation. "Let's play."

And we played silently for the next thirty minutes. After A.J. had won, I said I was ready for bed. He walked me to the window. I threw a leg over the sill and waited for him to kiss me goodbye.

He didn't.

I leaned over and gave him a peck on the cheek and made my way back to my own window.

We didn't say anything about that night all weekend. We did the usual—went to the railroad tracks and made out, went to the movies and held hands in the darkness—but we didn't say anything *important* to each other the whole time.

In August, A.J. and his dad left for a week to go up to Susquehanna. A.J. told me that the trip was coming up, but we didn't talk about what his going away to school would mean. For those four days I was pretty terrible. I snapped at Nancy, stayed mostly in my room when I wasn't at work, and didn't even read.

The one bright patch in those four days was Preston. Both A.J. and I had been neglecting him ever since we became a couple. I felt bad about that, but A.J. and I wanted as much time alone together as we could get. Preston kept asking to go to the movies with us, but we were always afraid that he would see us holding hands.

But before work on the morning of the third day that A.J. was gone, Preston texted ARE YOU DEAD?

Usually, he is more subtle.

I texted, NO. SORRY I HAVEN'T SEEN YOU.

He texted, CONTRARY TO EXPECTATIONS, I CONTINUE TO LIVE.

I NEVER EXPECTED OTHERWISE, I texted back.

DO YOU GUYS WANT TO DO SOMETHING TONIGHT? was the reply.

I wrote, A.J. OUT OF TOWN. I'M FREE. COME TO MY PLACE. 5:30?

His only reply was, THERE AND THEN.

That day at the cafeteria was unusually good. I was still bummed about A.J. not being there, but was very happy to be hanging with Preston again. One of the cronies of A.J.'s mom dropped me home that afternoon and I came upstairs to find Preston already waiting in my room.

He was in a dark pullover shirt that said STARFLEET on it, jeans and black sneakers. As we were approaching senior year of high school, Preston had grown a little taller and a little leaner. But there was still an adolescent…lumpiness to him that I thought he would soon grow out of. When I opened the door he looked up and gave me the Vulcan hand salute.

I tried to return it, but it usually came out with my fingers all crabbed and bent.

Preston smirked.

"Gimme a break," I said. "I speak it with an accent."

I came in and sat at my desk, pulling off my shoes. "I wanna shower first. I smell like a lunchroom. Then, whattaya wanna do?"

"Grammar lessons seem in order."

"Har-de-har-har." I grabbed a towel and some clothes from my drawer and told him to paw through my books while I cleaned up.

I went down the hall and showered and dressed. When I came back to my room, Preston was sitting there with a small bottle of soda. He pointed towards another one on my desk.

"Your mom says hello," he said.

"You went downstairs?"

"No," he said, sipping. "She brought them up."

"Oh," I said.

"She said with work and everything, she hardly gets to see you."

"Oh," I said, and grabbed the soda. "Want to hit a movie or goof off in the house?"

"Goof off," he said. "Nothing I want to see."

I grabbed the PlayStation and sat on the floor near him.

"Like your mom, I haven't seen you in ages."

"Been busy," I said.

"How's the romance?"

I looked at him.

"What romance?"

He laughed. It was rare, and it was more of a strangled ha-ha, but it was a laugh. "You and A.J."

"We're just friends."

He held up his palm, doing the Vulcan salute again. "Tell it to the hand."

I looked at him some more.

Then I gulped.

"Is it obvious?"

"Is what obvious?"

"You know," I said. "Do I seem…?"

His head inclined forward, like he was trying to figure out what I wanted to say.

"Do I seem…?"

He jumped right in. "Do you seem…gay? Is that it?"

I didn't answer. I just sipped my coke.

"What does it mean to seem gay?" he asked.

"You know," I said. "Gay."

"Are you gay?" he asked.

Oddly, it felt really good to talk about all of this. It made me feel unburdened, somehow. "I'm…I'm in love with A.J."

"That much is evident."

"It shows?"

"*That* again?"

"Jeez," I snapped. "Do you think you could talk like a normal guy for just a few minutes?"

He half-smiled. "I'm sorry. Really. It's just, I don't know what you're asking me."

"Do I seem gay to you?"

"No," he said. "But I have to add that I don't know what *seeming gay* means."

"Jeez," I repeated. "You know…gay."

"You seem like Thom," he said. "You seemed like Thom ten years ago and five years ago and ten minutes ago and right now. I don't think anybody is going to see you and say…*Hey, look, a homo.* They're going to say…*Hey, look, it's Thom.*"

I sipped my coke. "Am I gay?"

He actually shrugged. "How should I know?"

"You told me I was in love with A.J.!"

"Let me ask you this," he said. "If you weren't dating A.J., would you be dating another guy?"

"I never thought about it."

"Think about it."

I did.

"Are there other guys that you're attracted to?" he added.

I wondered if I should remind him that I tried to kiss him once. "Yes," I said. Really quiet. And looking at the floor.

"Then I'd guess yes," he said. "You're gay."

I didn't say anything.

"It could be worse," he said.

I didn't say anything.

"You could be a Denebian slime devil," he offered. "Or a nerf herder."

I looked at him. "You're a big help."

"I endeavor to provide satisfaction."

"Can you tell I'm in love with A.J.?"

"I *told* you," he said. "Remember?"

When I said nothing, he said, "So, to get back to the original question. How's the romance?"

"Good, I think."

"Are you happy?"

"Yes."

"Is he happy?"

"Yes," I said. "I think so."

"Think so?"

"Well...I'm not sure if he is completely comfortable being gay."

"Are you?"

"Not yet."

"Why should he be different?"

"Because."

"Hauntingly concise."

"What?"

"That means, *you sure are stupid*."

"Oh."

"Now you tell me something."

I lit up. "Sure."

"What's it like to be in love?" he asked.

"Duh," I said.

"What?" he asked.

"That means, *you sure are stupid*."

It may have been the first time anyone ever called him that.

"If I knew the feeling, I wouldn't have asked," he said.

"Haven't you ever been in love?"

"No."

"Preston," I started, then stopped. *Oh, hell*, I thought, and started again. "Preston, are you...gay?"

"No."

"Straight?"

He smiled. "Wouldn't you like to know?"

"But you've never been in love?"

"You know," he said, "You're the lucky one. Not everybody has what you have. Not everyone will ever have what you have. Never forget that."

That hit me. And hard.

"I guess I haven't been a good friend to you lately."

"Love affairs are usually exclusive."

"I wish you'd stop with the *love affairs* talk."

"Whatever," he said. "Do your folks know?"

"Mine don't."

"Sure?"

"Sure," I said. "At least...I think I'm sure."

"What about A.J.'s folks?"

"I think maybe his mom knows," I said. "But I'm not sure."

"You going to tell them?"

"No. Yes. I think so. Maybe."

"At least you have all the bases covered," he said. "You afraid?"

"Of telling?"

"Yes."

"Yes."

"Why?"

"Why not?"

"Do you think they'll love you less?"

"No. Yes. I think so. Maybe."

"*That* again."

"Have you talked to A.J. about all of this at all?" I asked.

"No."

I nodded.

"I think of both of you as my friends," Preston said. "But with A.J., it's different. He's much cooler than you are – and I don't mean that in a good way."

"Hey."

"Wait a minute. Let me finish. If he or I moved away he'd say *so long*, and seldom give me another thought. But I think you and I would stay in touch. You're the real friend to me."

"You think he'd do that to me?" I asked. "If I went away."

"He's in love with you."

"You think so?"

"I know so."

"How do you know?"

"When am I ever wrong?"

I had to give him that one.

"This is getting stale," he said, rising and stretching. "I've changed my mind. Let's hit the movies."

"I thought there was nothing you wanted to see."

"Who actually looks at the movie?" he asked. "The audiences are always more interesting."

"If you want."

"It's better than your staying here and whacking off to pictures of the Emperor of First Base."

"What makes you think I ever did that?"

He looked at me. "I'm a mind reader."

Somehow, I felt different about everything after that talk with Preston.

If I thought about anything at all, I thought that I was a guy who was in love with A.J. Lopez. But now, I got to thinking that I was a guy who also happened to be gay. It doesn't sound like much of a change, but it was.

I didn't mention my talk with Preston to A.J. And I don't know if Preston ever had a chance to discuss things with A.J.—if he did, neither of them ever mentioned it.

But it was a summer of firsts. First romance. First job. First…coming out, I guess, since I talked so honestly with Preston. It was also the summer we were able to drive alone and our first dance.

It happened like this.

When our July birthdays came, we were able to drive on our own now that we were seventeen, thanks to our taking Driver's Ed. Both sets of parents warned us to continue to be cautious. The whole Spike thing at this point was barely settling down, but I'm sure they wanted to keep us out of trouble.

I had started to read gay news sites online, and found out that Stony Brook University had a Gay-Lesbian-Straight Alliance. I wasn't quite sure what that was, but it sounded good to me. I read a lot about their activities on their site, and very soon after our birthdays I saw that they were having a dance. It was a "dry" dance, with no liquor allowed, and it promised to be "open".

Since our birthdays are two weeks apart, our folks had a joint party for us right between the two dates. Their big present was telling us that we were able to use the family cars, provided we "weren't stupid". A.J. also got a watch that his father made a big deal about. I got an iPad. That night, A.J. said he would've happily switched with me, but his dad would kill him. Mine would, too, so we just kept what we got.

We were coming home from work when I told him about the dance. I said it was nearby and we could leave early…no need to make trouble. I also said we could tell our folks we were going to the movies, if he wanted.

We were in his Toyota at that moment, with him driving. He didn't say anything at all after I asked, and when we paused at a STOP sign I asked, "Well?"

He leaned over and brushed his lips against mine. "I'd love to go dancing with you."

So, it was a date.

That night I told my folks that we were going to a dance at the college. They didn't ask any questions (which was good, as I didn't know what I'd say), and I got all dressed up. At first, I was confused. What did gay people wear? And…did I have to look different?

I texted A.J. and he said he was wearing jeans and a shirt. Seemed like a plan, but I actually ironed my jeans that afternoon. It was a first.

We took my family car this time (a sporty black all-electric Fiat, thank you very much), and we drove over to Stony Brook University. The event was in an auditorium behind the Student Union building, which we could find because it was near the cafeteria.

Even before we got close we could hear the music. As we approached the door, we could see guys and girls going in, most were a little older than us, but some were closer to our age. There was a student security guard at the door, but since it was liquor-free, he wasn't checking IDs.

We stood there, watching people go in. Neither of us had moved any closer.

Finally, the security guard looked up at us. "They ain't coming out here to meet you," he said.

I look at A.J. And then, just like that first day in kindergarten, he took my hand and led me inside.

The lights were flashing and the music was hot. The auditorium-turned-dance-floor was packed with people dancing. Guys dancing with guys. Girls dancing with girls. Guys and girls dancing. It was cool.

Neither A.J. nor I were big into music, and this was the first dance of any kind we had been to. We were mostly standing on the sidelines, watching, when he leaned over and kissed me on the ear.

I looked up at him.

He grinned and nodded towards the dance floor. Taking his hand we waded into the pool of people. Next thing you know, we were dancing.

We stank. I had no rhythm, and A.J. couldn't dance worth a darn. We didn't care. We weren't looking at our dance moves, anyway. We were looking at each other, falling more in love every moment. We were out dancing and all was right with our world.

We had danced to maybe ten songs when I thought I needed a breather. A.J. and I locked hands and went back to the sidelines, watching. There was a bar that sold juice and Cokes, and we snaked our way over.

A.J. left me at a good spot near the bar and went to get us some Cokes. I was standing there, watching the crowds, when a familiar face passed me.

I froze.

It was Robert Dillworth.

I didn't say anything. I figured if I stayed completely still, he wouldn't notice me. But, sure enough, he did. He turned just as I would've been out of the range of vision, and saw me. He smirked and came forward.

Dillworth never got as tall as me or A.J., but he still had broad and powerful shoulders and a thick neck. He had blond hair and dark eyebrows, and his face still looked like that of a handsome punk. I didn't know what to expect.

In seconds he was standing in front of me. He put out his fist and I bumped it (*That's familiar*, I thought). He turned and looked through the crowd.

Then he turned to me again. "I love this place," he said. "It's so gay."

I nodded.

Next thing you know, A.J. came over with our Cokes. When he saw Dillworth his face fell. He handed me my Coke, saying nothing.

Dillworth asked me, "Give a sip?"

Without thinking, I handed him my Coke.

He took a small pull and handed it back, head bopping to the music.

"So, you guys going together?"

"Yes," A.J. said. Strong and no hesitation.

"Cool."

More head bopping. Dillworth turns to me. "Hey, you mind if I dance once with A.J.?"

Me and A.J. exchange looks.

"If it's okay with A.J."

A.J. smiled at me. It was like he had just seen the best April Fool's joke in the world. He handed me his Coke and said, "Sure."

A.J. and Robert Dillworth stepped onto the dance floor. Dillworth was small and wiry, and I have to admit that he was a better dancer than either of us. They danced twice, and then came back to where I was standing, both sweaty.

A.J. took his drink and Dillworth just grabbed mine and took another sip.

"Keep it," I said.

We stood there, bopping to the music.

"So," I said to him. "Wanna dance?"

"No thanks," he said, surveying the crowd.

After a few minutes, he turned to A.J. "One more?"

A.J. looked at me for an OK. I nodded.

I took A.J.'s drink and they stepped out onto the dance floor again. Dillworth was in seventh heaven, but every now and then A.J. would shoot me a glance. I'd just smile and nod at him.

The rest of the night went on that way: me and A.J. dancing, then A.J. and Dillworth taking a turn. I didn't mind, A.J. was having fun and even Dillworth seemed almost human.

No wonder he wanted to hang out with A.J., I thought.

When it was getting time to head home, the three of us were by the drinks counter, having another Coke. Dillworth never treated for anything. But...I felt that this was the beginning of a new relationship for us. Better to forge it now than later.

"So, Bob," I said. "I'm glad to know we're part of the same community."

"What community?" His face was blank. Either he really didn't know, or he was expertly pulling my leg.

"You know," I said. "The LGBT community."

He looked at me in surprise, like I suddenly started speaking Hungarian.

"You know," I said. "The gay community."

His eyes got really narrow. "I'm not gay," he said. "I just like guys."

"Ah," A.J. said.

Dillworth looked at us both like we had just stolen the One Ring and were heading to Mount Doom.

"And if you say anything about this," he said to me, "I'll tear off your head and shove it up your ass."

I exchanged a look with A.J.

"Well," I said. "There's always that."

Chapter Ten

So, we became seniors.

Senior year is a year of big change for anyone. But me…it hit me hard.

Here's what happened.

Summer ended like it always does—with us wishing it would go on for another four months. We changed our summer jobs to after-school jobs, now working at the university cafeteria after a full day at St. John's.

Senior year is different to the first three. It's hard to explain, but it just is. You know you're leaving, and that's kind of exciting. And…you know you're leaving, and that's kind of sad.

For me, it was mostly sad because I was still worried about *what comes next*.

We ended up in the same homeroom for only the second time in four years (We were freshmen when we were last in the same homeroom). We didn't sit near one another, but we sure looked hard and long at each other. Preston was also in homeroom with us, and I would catch him reading our thoughts. When Preston jokes about reading minds, you never know whether to laugh or to be nervous.

Even Dillworth was in our homeroom. But he pretended that neither of us existed, much like always.

A.J. had taken up baseball again. He was such a superstar in junior year that the team never recovered from his defection. And while his love for the game returned, Spike forever remained *he who must not be named.*

Not that we ever had a chance to watch him again. Soon after our court date, Spike got suspended from the Majors and ended up in rehab. Whatever his demons were, they finally caught up with him.

I was doing really well at track. I'm still a powerfully built guy, no muscles like A.J., but solid like a tree trunk. I never picked up speed, but my endurance kept me a key part of the team.

After track and ball, whichever of us had use of a car would take the other to Stony Brook University. We would park as far away from the other cars as possible and kiss before heading into work. These were always the happiest moments of my day.

It was October, about a week before Halloween, and A.J. was driving us home from work when he said he wanted to go on a date.

"Great!" I said. "Where do you want to go?"

"Maybe dinner," he said. "Someplace nice where we could be alone."

"Wanna go to the city?"

I didn't think our folks would let us drive into Manhattan, but it didn't hurt to ask.

"No," he shrugged. "Someplace nearby. I'll think about it. How about Tuesday?"

That was two days before Halloween. St. John's was having a Halloween party for seniors' only, and I was looking forward to that. So, Tuesday was great.

When he pulled into his driveway I gave him a quick peck on the cheek and went in for dinner.

I was really excited about the date. Yeah, we saw each other every day and mostly had a chance to make out a couple of times a week. But that summer night we went to the Alliance dance was a turning point for me. Because that night was a date—something that we did in a planned way, rather than just because we were always together. It was something we specifically wanted, not just something that *happened*.

That weekend we piled through a lot of homework and grabbed pizza at a neighborhood place on Saturday night. Oh, and we spent a lot of Saturday kissing in my dad's car.

Sunday I had church (my mom still made me go) and I promised to drive Nancy to a movie. So it wasn't until Monday that he told me we were going to Compton's, a really nice restaurant not far from the college. He even told me that he had a reservation for us under my name—which was the first time I ever went anywhere I needed one.

Tuesday was a typical day: school, track/baseball, two hours at the University cafeteria. I drove us home that day and we split to shower and change before going out.

I had a good pair of dress slacks and I ironed a blue button-down shirt. Late October was getting pretty chilly, but I had a heavy navy blue corduroy jacket that I thought made me look pretty good. I texted, READY and went to sit in the car.

I was behind the wheel when he jumped in. I should've known right away that something was wrong, because his excitement level was low. He didn't even give me a peck on the cheek. He just said, "Let's go."

The trip didn't even take fifteen minutes. I had the radio playing as I drove.

"Maybe we could go dancing again," I said. "I checked online and there's another dance tomorrow, right before Halloween."

"That would be great," he said, but his voice was flat.

"We don't have to if you don't want to," I said. "We have the school party Thursday."

I parked in the rear and we went to the *maître d'* at the front desk and we were shown to a table.

I opened my jacket and sat. I have to admit it now, in a restaurant by candlelight, A.J. is almost impossibly handsome. I thought I was the luckiest guy in the world. It was a square table, so I sat at his right angle, rather than across from him. I smiled and grabbed his hand under the table.

"Dinner is my treat," he said.

"No, we should split it."

"No," he smiled at me. "Let me do this."

I shrugged.

Menus came and we looked through them. A.J. joked that menus are wasted on me, as I eat chicken whenever I get a chance. And that's what I ordered.

When the waitress left with our order, A.J. took my hand under the table.

"We need to talk."

"I don't like the sound of that."

"I was talking to my dad."

"You told him about us?"

"No," he said. "I mean, about college."

Now I was nervous. "Yes?"

"I got a scholarship from Susquehanna to play ball. I can go for a full scholarship, four years."

It felt like my face went numb.

"Are you going to go?"

He squeezed my hand tighter. "I have to."

"You're breaking up with me?"

"No," he said. And I could see the hurt in his brown eyes. "No. We'll visit. It'll just be a long-distance relationship."

I was staring at the bread on the table.

"Thom?" he asked.

I didn't say anything.

"Thom?"

"What do you want me to say?"

"That you forgive me."

"I love you."

"And I love you."

"*I'm* not going away."

"And *I'm* only going away for a little while."

"Four years!" I said. Loud. Real loud. People looked at us.

I went back to staring at the bread.

"Thom."

"What am I supposed to do for four years?"

"Go to school," he said. "Come visit me. Expect me to come visit you. Everything will be just the same. You just won't see me every day."

I took a drink of water. I looked at the tabletop and him not at all.

I felt his hand on my thigh and he held tight. I didn't say anything.

In a few minutes, our dinner came. A.J. looked down at his—pot roast with fries—and waited for me to respond.

"C'mon," he said. "It's getting cold."

I picked up my knife and fork and cut into my chicken and took a bite.

"Good?" he asked. Like he made it himself.

"Yeah," I said.

We ate for a little bit.

"I wouldn't have done this to you," I said.

"Thom," he said. "*Please.* You think I want to go?"

"Then why are you doing it?"

"It's a *scholarship*," he said, like I didn't hear him the first time. "They'll pay for nearly everything. When I told my dad, he said there was no way we could turn it down."

I cut another piece of meat, but left it on my plate.

"And what about the rest of the year?"

"This year?"

"Yeah, asshole," I said, instantly regretting it. "The rest of this year."

He sat up a little straighter. I meant to hurt him, and I did. He just ate for a few minutes without talking.

Now I took his hand under the table.

"I'm sorry."

"It's okay," he said.

"What about the rest of this year?" I asked again.

"Nothing changes," he said. "Why should it?"

224

I didn't have a reason. But, suddenly, it felt like *everything* had changed.

I don't know how long people spend in Compton's, but we must've set some kind of record. I think we were finished with dinner, paid and out in just a little over thirty minutes.

When we were heading back to the car, A.J. asked, "Want to do something else? Find a movie? Or maybe see if there is something going on at the Alliance at the college?"

I opened the door and slid behind the wheel. "Thanks," I said. "Can't. Homework."

He opened the passenger door and climbed in.

I took the keys and tried to put them in the ignition, missing a few times. Suddenly, his hand closed around mine.

"Thom," he said. "Stop."

I looked at him. I don't think my face was friendly.

"Thom," he said.

Then he wrapped his arms around me and I held him tightly.

"Sorry," I said.

"No," he said, "I'm sorry."

"I just don't want you to go."

"Don't take it like this, Thom," he said, his voice a whisper against my ear. "I'll stay if you want. I'll turn it down."

"I don't want you to do that," I said. I took my arms from him and gripped the steering wheel. "When do you have to tell them?"

"I already told them," he said. "But I can change my mind."

"You *already* told them?"

"Yeah."

"Oh." It wasn't such a big word, but it hung in the air.

"Well," I added. "I'm not mad. But I really do want to go home. I'm beat."

He kissed me again. "Okay. Just let me know what you want me to do."

So, I drove us home.

When I pulled into the driveway, he gave me a quick kiss and said, "Love you" before vanishing into his house.

Home, Mom and Dad were listening to music in the living room. Mom smiled when I came in.

"Hey, I thought you guys were having a night on the town," Dad said.

"Just tired," I said, heading for the stairs.

"Everything okay?" Mom called after me.

"Fine," I said, reaching my door. "Night."

I peeled off my clothes and got into sweatpants and a shirt. I looked across at A.J.'s window. I didn't see him there, but his light was on. I locked my window—which may be a first—and turned off my light before climbing into bed.

That morning I was supposed to take A.J. to school and work. After showering, dressing and breakfast I climbed into the car and left on my own.

My phone beeped when I got to school. It was a text from A.J.

Forget something?

I paid no attention.

Somehow he got to school on time. He was nearby in homeroom, but I studiously avoided him. I don't know what brain waves Preston was picking up, because I decided to ignore Mr. Spock, Jr., too.

After homeroom I went to my first class. I half expected A.J. to follow and stop me, and was both surprised and disappointed when he didn't.

I did track as usual and went home on my own. When I got home I found another text from A.J.

Asshole.

I didn't answer.

I ate at home that night and I guess I wasn't good company again (I seemed to be making a habit of that). Mom and Dad just wrote off my moodiness to school or being tired, but Nancy was more perceptive. She was nearly fifteen now, and still a brat.

"Mom," she said. "Thom is upset."

"No, I'm not."

Dad looked up from dinner. "Thom? You unhappy?"

"No!"

"Nancy, eat your dinner," Mom said.

"You sure?" Nancy asked.

"I'm sure," Mom said.

"I mean Thom."

"I'm sure," I said, looking daggers at her.

"Tomorrow's the Halloween thing at school, right?" Mom asked.

"Yeah."

"You going?"

"I guess."

"With A.J.?"

I looked up at that. "I don't know if I'm going."

"But I thought you were waiting for it all week?"

"I don't know if I'm going!"

My dad looked up at that.

"So don't go," he said. "You don't have to."

I mumbled something.

"What was that?" my dad asked.

"I said, *that's right.*"

***

Halloween.

The day dawned dull, dark, gray and soundless. I climbed out of bed and showered and dressed, coming down to breakfast on a morning that looked little different from the evening. I didn't know if I was going to school, or to the House of Usher.

Mom was gone that day—taking the train to see some cronies in the city. No one was in the kitchen other than Nancy. Now that she was in high school herself, she was less of an irritant—probably because she had a whole passel of friends of her own to annoy. As I poured myself a cup of coffee, this morning she decided to revert to form.

"You look lousy," she said.

"Thanks."

"You didn't sleep?"

"Don't you have a house to haunt?"

She sipped her cup of tea. "Well, it's Halloween. You're really not going to the party tonight?"

"I haven't made up my mind."

"You have a fight with A.J.?"

That got my attention. "You know not every moment of my life is devoted to A.J."

"Don't get sore."

"I'm not sore."

"Then why is your face red?"

I mumbled some words that won't be repeated here and grabbed my books and went to the car.

A.J. and I didn't text, so we had no plans to share the ride. At homeroom I ignored him, though I could see him looking at me now and then. When the bell rang, I raced for my next class.

I'm fast, but not as fast as Preston. Before I made it to my next class, my phone went *ping*.

It was from Preston. EVERYTHING ALRIGHT WITH YOU AND A.J.?

I just had time before the class-starting bell to text, MIND YOUR OWN BUSINESS, ASSHOLE.

Preston didn't answer.

Clearly not my best moment. At the rate I was shutting people out, I'd be left with no one but my sister. And what fun that would be…

Somehow I got through the day. I had to answer a couple of questions in calculus at the board, which I did with really bad grace. I don't know if my grouchiness was written off as teenage bad behavior or just Halloween goofiness, but no one called me on it.

I skipped track that day and went home. The lights were off and I thought I had the house to myself. I came in the front door and threw my books on the couch before heading to my room.

"Hey, son."

It was Dad. He was in the den and was probably working on a cartoon. He had a small lamp over a drawing table, no wonder I thought the house was dark. He was dressed in his standard-issue uniform of a rumpled cardigan and khakis.

"Hi," I said.

"How was school?"

I tried the raising-one-eyebrow trick. Haven't done it in a while, it still works. He just smiles as if I had said something rude.

"You going to the Halloween party?"

"No."

Silence.

"You okay?"

"Yeah."

More silence.

"Okay," he said.

I turned and headed upstairs. I kicked off my sneakers and was sitting on the bed when there was a knock at the door. Before I could answer, my dad was opening it standing there.

"What's wrong?" he asked.

"Nothing."

He came over and sat on the bed next to me. "Don't lie to your old man."

I couldn't help it. My eyes got leaky and tears started rolling down my cheeks. They felt hot.

Dad put an arm around me and hugged me. Then he let go. "C'mon. Give."

So, wiping my face, I told him about me and A.J. About how we were in love, and had been dating. About being gay and how I knew that I would like guys, whether it was A.J. or someone else. And about how much A.J. meant to me and how I felt about his leaving for school. Then, I told him about the fight we had at Compton's and how I wasn't talking to him.

Dad, he never said a word. After I got it all out, he squeezed my knee.

"So?" I asked.

"Yeah?"

"Don't you have anything to say?"

"About what?"

"About me being gay?"

He actually smiled, which made me mad for a moment. "You don't think it's a surprise, do you?"

"It's not?"

"I am your dad, you know. At this point I think I know you pretty well."

My eyes were wet again—how I hate that. "Do you still love me?"

He actually laughed. Now I *was* mad.

"It's not funny!"

He put an arm around me. "Well…what's funny is asking if I still love you. *Of course* I still love you. You're my son. I'll always love you."

I was wiping my face with the back of my hand.

"You *are* stupid, though," he added. Leave it to my dad.

"What?"

"Well, far be it for me to interfere in your love life, but I don't think you're being fair to A.J."

"He's *leaving*!"

"He's going to college," Dad corrected. "You've known each other all your lives. If you really do love one another, I think it'll survive being apart for college. And it's not like you won't see him. You'll visit."

Silence.

"Is A.J. going to this Halloween thing?"

I nodded.

"You should go and find him," Dad said. "Apologize and make nice. You only have a little less than a year together before he goes to school."

"You think?"

"I know," he said. "But first, I want you to come with me to the train station. I'm picking up Mom and I don't want to be the one to tell her."

"I have to tell her today?"

He stood and reached out a hand. "C'mon."

It was raining full-bore now and Dad and I dashed to the car. He drove and I took the back seat so Mom could sit up front. We got to the depot and parked, the rain drumming on the car top. We were just in time to see the train pull in. Dad checked his phone, answered a text from Mom, and in seconds she jumped into the passenger seat.

She gave Dad a peck on the check and turned to look at me. Then she turned to look at Dad. Our faces must've been something.

I started crying.

"Oh, God," she said. "Who's dead?"

"No one's dead," Dad said. "He told me he's gay and he wanted you to know too."

"Oh," my mother said. She turned to Dad. "You make dinner?"

"No," he said. "We're dropping him off at the Halloween party and then I'll take you for Chinese."

"Wait a minute!" said I.

Mom turns. "Yes?"

"I'm gay."

"Yes, dear."

"Well?"

"Well…it's not like it's a surprise."

"I'm dating A.J."

"And…?"

Well, she had me there.

"Sweetheart, I love you a lot."

"I love you too."

My mother turned to my father. "That was easier than I expected."

We all chatted for the next few minutes as Dad took me to St. John's. Seems that they had figured out I was gay a long time ago (I wonder if Preston told them...? *Nah*). And they kinda, sorta, maybe figured that A.J. and I had become a couple...but weren't sure. And as for A.J., as Mom said, "It's not like we don't know him already."

They pulled in front of St. John's and Mom handed me her collapsible umbrella. I kissed them both and Dad said, "Don't do anything stupid."

And I stepped out into the rain and watched the car pull away.

I went into the school and navigated to the gym, where the party was being held. On the way I ran into Preston. When he saw me, he kept walking.

I ran up to him and grabbed his arm.

"Preston!"

He gave me a stony look.

"You know what? I'm the asshole." I put out my hand. "Truce?"

He didn't take my hand. Instead, he gave me the Vulcan salute. And then he said, "Live long, and prosper."

I couldn't help it. I hugged him. Then I went looking for A.J.

I went to the gym that had been converted for the senior Halloween party. There were black and orange lights and really loud music and tables everywhere with real food (chicken and stuff) and candy. There were even booths for games, both electronic and real (like tossing little bean bags into holes, go figure). Several teachers were there along with a handful of parents.

I look around. I see Dillworth, mouthing off to a teacher after he missed a beanbag toss. I see some of the guys from religion class, and all the math nerds huddled together.

And then I caught sight of A.J. He was standing off near the bleachers, a couple of guys on the ball team standing around him like they were warming their hands at his fire.

I nearly ran up to him.

I was almost on top of him before he saw me. Without a word, I took him by the hand—just like he took me by the hand that first day in kindergarten. I led him out of the gym, the ballplayers standing there, looking open-mouthed as we left.

I took A.J. through the hall, out the door, and then out into the rain.

It was pouring. Water was running down our faces, in seconds, our hair was plastered to our scalps.

"I'm sorry," I said.

He looked at me, water running off his face.

"I love you," I said.

He stood there, looking at me in the rain. Then he said: "I love you too."

We wrapped our arms around one another and kissed.

Chapter Eleven

So, what comes next?

Well, what came immediately next is that we were drenched and had to go home and change.

The rest of that year was interesting. Parts of it were hard—it soon got around that A.J. and I were dating, and not everyone at St. John's was happy about that. But, it was all a whole lot less drama than I expected. And, for what it's worth, Robert Dillworth came out too. He punched some guy who tried to make fun of him, and somehow, that made the topic off limits.

When we graduated, A.J. got a medal for baseball. I think I should've gotten one for religion, but lost out. I did score one for English though.

We worked that summer in the Stony Brook University cafeteria again. I was going there that coming September, and had already started making friends at the Gay-Lesbian-Straight Alliance. (Preston said it sounded like part of the Galactic Empire. But that's Preston.)

Speaking of Preston, he got medals in every subject except gym. He was leaving at the end of summer to go to

Princeton for pre-med courses. I told him to work on his bedside manner.

Other than that, A.J. and I spent the rest of our time together, quietly and tenderly in love with one another. I don't know if he ever told his parents…but, like my folks, how could they not know? Maybe they were waiting for A.J. to tell them himself. At any rate, his parents never treated me any differently for the remainder of the year, and that made me happy.

That last full day in August we took off from work and just moped around town together. I'm not sure how it happened, but we ended up at the railroad tracks near Preston's home, and were walking on the slats between the rails, holding hands.

When I saw the clump of trees where we first kissed, I pulled him towards them and we held one another.

While there, A.J. said this: "Whatever happens, I know I will never be loved like I am loved by you."

As for what comes next? I have no idea.

Everything, so far, has taken me by surprise.

Acknowledgements

No book is written in a vacuum. Many thanks to my agent, Tom Cull, and to my editor, David Baclaski, for having such faith in me over the years. Thanks to Rowan Thomas, my editor at Vulpine, for making this a better book. Thanks to my brother David Lee Madison, who introduced me (kicking and screaming) to baseball. Thanks to all my first readers: Claudia Fitzpatrick, Isadora Frost, Jessica Griffith, Amanda Stacy Madison and Mike Machnik. Finally, thanks to the two most important people in my life: Russell (the husband!) and Lucas (the dog!).

Bob Madison is a former communications executive turned writer. He has written everything from magazine articles, blogposts, television documentaries, nonfiction books, cookbooks, novels and even…trading cards. Bob Madison has been married to Russell Frost since 1990, and the two live in Huntington Beach, CA. Bob currently sits on the board for The Literacy Volunteers of Huntington Beach Public Library.

Contact him on Twitter: @thatbobmadison,
or visit his website: www.thatbobmadison.com.